A WORK OF ART

A WORK OF ART

and other stories

Denys Val Baker

WILLIAM KIMBER · LONDON

First published in 1984 by
WILLIAM KIMBER & CO. LIMITED
100 Jermyn Street, London, SW1Y 6EE

ISBN 0-7183-0524-8

Photoset in North Wales by
Derek Doyle & Associates, Mold, Clwyd
Printed in Great Britain by
Biddles Ltd, Guildford and King's Lynn

Contents

I

A Work of Art

1

I have sometimes – in the dark hours of the night or perhaps while striding in glorious solitude over some bleak and lonely Cornish landscape (*her* landscape) – wondered just how it all began. Now when it is too late for the benefits of any such wisdom I can answer the question exactly.

I suppose in a way it began for me at the very start of my own love affair with Cornwall on that day when leaning out of the window of the sleek Cornish Riviera express, I looked down upon the swirling waters of the River Tamar and realised with a strange and lingering excitement that I was crossing the border into another land, a new country. Cornwall was like that to me from the first, a place apart; certainly from the moment I glimpsed the forlorn humps of Bodmin Moor, rearing massively against the vast sky, and again when later I caught my first glimpse of the sea washing its way into the very soul of the land, huge waves frothing and surging against the granite rocks ...

After I had moved into the bungalow I had rented on the moors above St Ives and settled into the life of the art colony it was inevitable that sooner or later I would be drawn to the work of the local painters – and finally, but yes I can see irrevocably, to *her* work, the inspired work of that creature of genius who somehow by instinct captured all the mysteries and marvels to which I had to come by a more laboured route.

It was that work and not her name or her self which first captured my attention and fired my imagination. I might well

7

have come across it in one of the larger galleries, the Penwith at St Ives or the Passmore Edwards Gallery by the sea at Newlyn – but in fact it was elsewhere that all that vivid colour and unexpected sensuality first blazed into my world. As anyone who has visited St Ives will be aware, the town retains many of the characteristics of an old fishing port, most especially the narrow confinement of cobbled streets and huddled fishermen's cottages winding up the steep hill from the sea. I found myself wandering along on an afternoon when an enveloping Cornish mist had seeped in from seawards, casting its dampening effects into every nook and cranny. Suddenly in the centre of a large display window of a small art gallery that had obviously been converted from a former fish loft, my attention was seized by a veritable blaze of colours, a large painting splashed and daubed and shining as brightly as the golden sun itself.

I can still remember the astonishment with which I stopped in my tracks and the momentary nervousness (in case it proved an illusion) with which I stepped nearer to the window to see this apparition more clearly – above all the incredulity with which I recognised that my discovery was indeed just that, a discovery, a revelation, an introduction to something which then, and indeed to this day, perhaps, I found a little awe-inspiring. A new, no, more, a *unique*, talent.

I am a writer, not a painter or an art critic and no doubt my attitude to painting would be what is called literary, i.e. rather on the romantic side: indeed I must confess I did not know then and have never bothered to ascertain since, exactly what standard of technical abilities lay behind the painting I now gazed upon in that alley gallery window. All I knew was that the vivid scattered combinations – colours and shapes, lines and shadows, sea and land and sky all concentrated into some cohesive whole – exploded outwards towards me with all the effect, one might imagine, of a gunshot. Yes, quite literally, that painting blasted itself into my existence: once I had seen it I had the sensation I would never again be able to view any Cornish landscape with quite the same innocent eyes.

It was a painting which managed somehow to capture not

merely a single element of what might be called the true Cornwall – but, I would swear, *all* the elements. Here was not merely the land, the twisted, often grotesque, granite shapes burrowing into limitless depths of earth – not just the eternal restless image of the sea beyond, vast clouds of spray and spume frothing up into the air – not even merely the huge canopy of the pale skies above, bright blue flickering through jostling white clouds – no, there was much more besides. Upon the sea, symbol of mankind's minute place in the universe, there tossed a single forlorn Cornish lugger, its bright red sail leaning at an angle – somewhere against the moorland background there reared the crumbling finger of an old mine chimney-stack, relic of mankind's failure – even in the sky itself there were hints of a strange immortality, whispers of other worlds whose secret shadows, in Cornwall, are always particularly evident.

I don't know how long I stood transfixed, staring into that gallery window, but it must have been for quite a period for when I emerged from a kind of daze I found that the lingering Cornish mist had seeped into my jacket so that it was quite damp. Also my interest must have aroused attention inside for an elderly gentleman with a beard appeared in the doorway and cast towards me an inquiring smile. There was about him all the air of someone about to ask if I might be interested and if so, etc.

Not wishing to be rudely awakened from my dreamy contemplation I turned brusquely and hurried away down the alley – escaping from possible cross-examination, but of course taking with me forever the wild memory of the blazing slash of bright colours.

From then onwards I became as a man haunted – haunted at first by a single image, but before long by others for naturally, wishing to assuage my curiosity, I soon began looking around for further examples of work by this same marvellous painter.

In this matter I must admit that in the long run the elderly bearded man was to prove most helpful. When I returned to the gallery less dazed and more able to make inquiries he readily responded – no doubt with an eye to the future – when indeed I was to prove a valuable customer. It appeared that he had been one of the first to discover this remarkable new talent: – that was why, he explained, although now that she was becoming known her work was in all the better galleries, he was still privileged to display several contemporary examples. Perhaps I would like to see the ones that even now were hanging inside his little gallery?

And so, not without some nervousness, I allowed myself to enter a little further into this new and magical world. Inside the gallery there was a mixed exhibition, including several quite interesting works by other local artists, but my eyes were at once drawn to the now familiar blaze of colours. Cornwall is in fact generally a place of greyness and granite but this very drabness of background often serves to emphasise all the more any occasional splash of colour, and it was like that with these paintings. There was a view of the sun sinking behind Clodgy Point, for instance, that captured all the marvellous burning flames associated with such an event – yet at the same time, too, hinted at the stunningly beautiful green of the cliff tops, at the sea-washed, almost bony white of the great sands of Porthmeor below.

It was a marvellous work, it seemed to me, one which the more I examined the more I coveted – and in fact it became the very first of those paintings which I purchased, that casual summer afternoon in the little back-street gallery in St Ives. Perhaps because fame had not yet quite arrived, the price was a very reasonable £50. I wrote a cheque and the bearded gentleman carefully wrapped the painting up in brown paper and handed it over for me to carry back to my faraway bungalow.

And it was only there, some hours later, all by myself in the small but cosy sitting room holding the painting up against the granite wall and deciding on just the best position, above the fireplace where I knew I could see it easily every time I looked up from my writing table over by the window – it was only there and then that at last I had the curiosity to take my gaze away from the painting itself and to search for the identity of the artist, scrawled rather indefinitely in a remote corner of the painting but printed more clearly and exactly on the back. Her name at last: *Victoria Amanda Hosking*.

Even so for a long time it was neither the name nor the possible personality of the painter which interested me and my attention remained captured totally and almost hypnotically by the paintings themselves. Perhaps in order to provide some sort of explanation for what transpired later I should try and give the reader a clearer idea of just what type of paintings they were. To begin with they were quite unlike any other paintings I had ever seen: this I mean sincerely, and I have visited quite a few well known art galleries in my time. Glimpses of other painters there were, of course. Turner, for example, that genius of sea paintings – Van Gogh, that other genius who captured the land in all its brilliant colours – even more modern painters like Braque and Picasso, yes traces of them, too. But in the long run, when it was down to a painting in its solitary splendour, then each one seemed unique.

Perhaps one of the reasons for this was the elusive way in which they defied any sort of categorisation. They were landscapes, yes – but in no way could you describe them as conventionally so. They were naturalistic and yet sometimes they could be seen as the opposite, as abstract. Looked at in another way they managed somehow to combine exact observation with strangely blurred execution, an impressive achievement – gazing upon a picture, one became totally convinced of the scene and yet aware of hints of strangeness. Superficially one might have described most of the paintings as landscapes yet the fact was that each one appeared to possess a strange life of its own as if – well, as if in a way the view was a *living* thing.

And this brings me, finally, to the most remarkable feature of all – the disturbing sensuality underlying every painting, incorporated it often seemed into every brushstroke – sensuality or sexuality, call it what you will, the impact was the same. Looking upon the vistas of land and sea, sky and rock, moors and cliffs, one was constantly impressed by a sense of swirling movement, of slumbering strengths – as of limbs about to break into strange erotic movements.

Have I explained the paintings? Of course not, you would have to see them even to begin to understand. But I, well I *could* see them, and as time went on saw more and more of them – indeed, over a period bought a further half a dozen. Soon they stood about my bungalow, filling it to bursting with their powerful illuminations ... Coming in from a walk on the cliffs, especially if there had been one of those overcast skies or straggling mists, was like entering a new and magical kingdom, a world I had never known before. A world, I began to reflect, given to me as a present by this strange, unknown being: *Victoria Amanda Hosking*.

I suppose that was when at last my curiosity shifted from paintings to the painter, from the act to the creator. I learned that unlike many local painters she was Cornish and had lived all her life in West Penwith. Apart from a year or two at Art School she was self taught. In her early thirties, she was apparently unmarried, and so on ...

Looking back I can see there was a sort of inevitability about the process. Soon it seemed only natural that I should be drawn to the person as much as to her work – indeed, that I would surely fall in love with the person with the same totality and passion as I had fallen in love with her creations. In a small community like the St Ives art colony it would not normally take long to get to know certain individuals, especially someone in the public eye. However Victoria Amanda Hosking, though she exhibited in the St Ives and Penzance galleries, did not live in either town, but somewhere out in the wilds near Land's End. For this reason, then, my first encounter with her was some time in arriving – and when it did happened to be accidental and very fleeting, though none the less remarkable for all that.

I had by then joined the Penwith Arts Society as a lay member and so regularly received invitations to their exhibitions. In due course there came a private viewing of the big annual summer show, and so on a lovely sunlit evening I came into St Ives, leaning first over the rails at the Malakoff and watching the dolls' houses lining the harbour far below, toy boats bobbing around, then walking through the bustling

little port and down to Downalong where among the
fishermen's cottages the Penwith had built their long granite
gallery. When I went in there was quite a crowd there,
including a few local painters and potters I had come to know
through conversations in the Sloop and the Castle. To some of
them I nodded, now and then stopping to chat briefly, but all
the time my eyes were searching around ... Ah, yes, *there* was
one of her paintings – and there, my word, *there* was a huge
one, it must have measured six feet square in all, one of the
showpieces of the exhibition, surely, a glorious and exotic view
of a lonely carn high up on a bleak stretch of moorland.

I went over and stood taking in the full effect of the painting,
marvelling as ever at its elusive effects. After a while, sensing
that several other people were anxious to look, I stood further
back and began to look around with some curiosity. Surely at
such an occasion the painter herself might be present?

I can remember that particular evening looking quite
specifically at quite a few of the visitors – painters in smocks or
jeans, other more sprucely dressed individuals whom I guessed
to be local business people – oh, and quite a few students, too.
Sometimes there was an interesting figure, a splash of colour
that caught the eye, and I found myself wondering – would
that be her?

After a while I had to shrug to myself rather helplessly. How
would I ever know? I turned back to look at the picture again.
Just at that moment I saw someone emerge from the shadows
behind me, someone who, too, had obviously been studying
the crowds, watching the people as they looked at the picture.
As I stood politely to one side I saw that the shadowy figure
was in fact a woman, perhaps in her late thirties, with the dark
almost Spanish looks which are often found in the Cornish.
She was dressed in a subdued fashion, but this in a way
heightened the most striking thing about her – the long dark
hair, flowing back over her shoulders, lending to her a
strangely romantic appearance. She was not, a detached
observer might have decided, by any means beautiful or even
conventionally pretty – yet there *was* something about her, the
way she held herself and moved – above all that striking dark

hair with its accompanying aura of hidden mystery –
something that made you feel physically aware, once seen not
easily forgotten.

Because I had stood to one side the woman glanced
momentarily in my direction, and for the first time I saw her
full face, met briefly the gleam of her dark eyes. I suppose I
may have romanticised it all and yet in the first glance did I not
just for a moment capture a fleeting look of something,
perhaps even recognition? – of some fellow spirit? Certainly I
felt so on my own part – and her? What did she think?

Then she was gone, disappearing round the corner and then
out of the building itself. She seemed to be alone, as indeed so
often she was to seem …

I hurried over to the secretary's desk.

'Excuse me, that lady who just left – can you tell me who she
was?'

The secretary looked over her shoulder, and smiled.

'That was Victoria Amanda Hosking. You know – '

'Yes,' I said slowly. 'Yes, I know.'

2

Would I ever really know Victoria Amanda Hosking? I could
not help wondering despondently about the possibility in the
days following the Penwith opening. Now that, even though so
elusively, I had glimpsed the painter herself, the reality behind
the works of art, I was conscious of a subtle shift in the focus of
interest. Still when I awoke each morning it was my sensual
delight to walk around looking at her paintings, *my* possessions
– mine to touch and fondle, to gaze upon with all the greedy
pleasure of an owner. But now, unmistakably, there were other
emotions, too, a feeling of curious limitation – of possessing
and yet not possessing, of owning a picture but not perhaps its
soul?

Whatever the strange and perhaps instinctive reasoning
going on in my head during those days there could be no

doubt as to the direction in which it was leading me. Buying and thereby apparently possessing not merely one but half a dozen of the paintings was not enough. It was suddenly imperative to get much closer, to enter much more deeply into that secret world – indeed to *know* Victoria Amanda Hosking.

For a long time I seemed unable to make any progress in this ambition. Once or twice at other art shows I caught a glimpse of the elusive lady but that was all it was – the most fleeting of contacts yet again, time only for me to observe one or two more features about her – the way she had of suddenly holding her head up quickly, just like a wild bird can be seen to do – another habit she had of brushing her long hair away from her forehead and back over her shoulders, as if somehow trying to curb some wayward tendency that lurked within her innermost being – yes, I noted that sort of item. But they were merely part of the outer veneer, I still did not know the woman at all. My one consolation was that by the very nature of the brief encounters she herself must have been at least made aware of my existence. I can remember the briefest exchange of glances, just for a moment the stray glimpse of a curious gaze on her part at this new face of someone patently more than mildly interested.

Often after one of these encounters I would feel impelled to return to my bungalow there to stand pensively before those familiar splashes of colour as if somehow by gazing long enough at the painting I would somehow see further into the being of their creator. But this was not to be, I realised. More than once I stormed out in a fit of frustration and anger, stamping away over the wild moors around me.

It was after such experiences, strangely enough, that I found myself beginning to write a series of stories I had been vaguely planning – about Cornwall itself, about its effects upon people who, like myself, came down and fell under its spell. On such occasions I noticed that the writing seemed to come easily and indeed fluently, and sometimes I became excited as I read back what I had written. There was no doubt that some of my paragraphs did seem to capture something of Cornwall's mysterious, brooding character.

Eventually it was such experiences that gave me the idea for finding a way to get to know Victoria Amanda Hosking. If my stories were even moderately successful in their aim – how much more so would they be if they could benefit from being illustrated by such an artist?

At first I felt too nervous to pursue the idea: after all she might regard it as presumptuous on my part to make such a suggestion. But in the end, as frustrating day after frustrating day went by and I remained with a sense of being in limbo, I forced myself into action. From the secretary of the Penwith Society I obtained Victoria Amanda Hosking's address, and one momentous day I sat down and wrote her my first letter. I wrote, of course, most tactfully, merely inquiring in the first instance if she might remotely be interested in my proposition but emphasising what an honour I would regard it if she would consider it. Even more nervously I enclosed two of my stories for her inspection.

The next few days seemed to drag interminably. Each morning I rushed to meet the postman cycling along the passing lane, only each time to be disappointed. Then at last, one week later, there came a reply – brief even terse but all important, suggesting that the best thing would be for me to come out and have a chat.

So at last I came to meet Victoria Amanda Hosking. I can remember the occasion well for it was one of those glorious Cornish summer days when the sky was one vast blue dome, the sun shimmering in its centre and casting its magical rays of warmth upon land and people alike, awakening us all to a feeling akin to ecstasy – oh, a day it was good to be alive on!

I had discovered that Victoria lived in an old cottage on the outskirts of a remote village on the very tip of the Land's End peninsula. I drove there along winding and torturous lanes that eventually plunged downward until I found myself looking out upon a marvellous view of the Atlantic stretching out for miles – in the distance just visible, the long finger of the Wolf lighthouse, one of the beacons guarding the entrance to the English Channel. The cottage itself stood out starkly against the skyline, perched almost incredibly on the very top of the cliffs with breathtaking views all around, yet looking as if it had always existed, as if like the granite boulders all around it had literally grown up from secret hidden depths.

When I had parked in a field below and climbed the steep path leading to the cottage I found my host waiting for me at the porch. At first sight she seemed as enigmatic a figure as ever, but at least now she was not passing me fleetingly but indeed ready at last to regard me with a curious gaze, even, dared I hope, with some interest?

'I've read your stories. You've managed to get quite a feeling of place.'

She shrugged – ah, that shrug! I was to come to know it so well!

'But I don't think, you know, I could actually illustrate them. Anyway, come in … '

She ushered me into a tiny entrance hall and then up a shadowy staircase at the top of which a door opened upon a marvellous flood of light. I found myself inside her studio, obviously two former rooms knocked into one, with the whole of one wall fitted with picturebook windows so that everywhere was flooded with sunlight and one felt indeed washed by the very elements.

'What a marvellous position!'

'I like it, yes. It's where I do all my best work, I fancy.'

As she spoke she waved a hand around indicating some of the paintings that lay scattered around in their varying blazes of colour.

'Some of my latest work. That's what I was going to say – I didn't mean to sound too disappointing, but you see I cannot face doing any *specific* illustrations. That's not the way I work anyway – however it struck me maybe you could pick out some of my paintings and we could get those photographed and use them for illustrations?'

That was what we decided upon, quite quickly and without fuss. And then, as we sat over a cup of coffee, I began nervously, my first overtures to Victoria Amanda Hosking. She was not, I soon discovered, the purely romantic creature I had imagined in my earlier glimpsings: about painting and the art world generally she had a very pragmatic attitude. She had no illusions about her own worth, which she rightly put highly and she was obviously determined to look after her own interests in a businesslike way. But that said, she retained about her a certain quality of elusiveness, even of remoteness.

I suppose whatever sort of character I had encountered I would have been inclined to dramatise the meeting – as it was, meeting in that romantically situated studio, surrounded by dozens of those marvellous paintings whose mysteries had for so long dominated my life – against such a background even if the woman herself had been plain and ordinary I would have been drawn irresistibly towards her. And plain and ordinary she was not, but – a little like her paintings – sensually alive, a creature of physical purpose and meaning whose very presence in a room compelled one to a new awareness.

In short, and no doubt inevitably, from that first morning I fell under the sway of Victoria Amanda Hosking the woman, just as already I had become completely possessed by her paintings. To put it another way, I fell in love.

3

In some ways I was lucky on the occasion of that first momentous meeting. Because it was such a lovely day there was an almost irresistible urge to be out among the elements. After a while Victoria picked up her sketching pad and some pencils and said she would be going out along the cliffs. I do remember now that she never specifically invited me to accompany her but then she did not forbid me either. And so I followed her rather meekly, the first of many such processions. Perhaps, I cannot possibly be sure now, perhaps she had not meant me to go, but anyway once I was there she seemed prepared to chatter away, not about herself, indeed, but certainly about her work.

'I've thought a lot about why Cornwall attracts painters. It's this crystal-clear light – it gives everything a new meaning, the form and structure of the landscape is defined and enlarged. And then the atmosphere – it's so extraordinary, stimulating, savage, strong, primitive, beautiful.'

As she spoke, throwing the words out almost casually, she climbed lithely up and up a steep path that took us into a world of heather and thyme and long granite-flaked slopes – and behind her I clambered more laboriously, my ears filled with those words and their images – savage, strong, primitive, beautiful. When we got to the top and settled on a protruding granite shoulder I could not resist every now and then looking sideways at my companion – and yes, I could believe she was all these things as she sat there completely engrossed in what she was doing, her body arched forward as if indolently to outline its hidden charms, the long dark hair periodically being swept back impatiently, making a frame to the half hidden face, now bent down upon the task of drawing some distant view of the sea.

Later we walked on along the cliffs, following a path that took us to the very end of the coastline, where the southern cliffs turned and became the western cliffs, the spot marked by what I suppose must be the 'first and last' coastguard station in England. Here we stood on a flat slab of granite that existed almost like a platform for stepping into some other world.

'Words are really inadequate, aren't they?' She looked suddenly pensive and then her face seemed to clear. 'The most important part of it all to me is this mysterious X an artist must *feel* about a place to paint and be true to his art. There's the shimmering of pale bleached grasses, surging half-seen rocks, mist, rain, storm, sun on moors and headlands, and of course, skies and skies ... that's part of what I try to paint.

'For me the seas and moors and skies and rocks of Cornwall are inexhaustible material. Then always there's this peculiar clarity of light, throwing the landscape of West Penwith into perspective. It's a land of great antiquity, primeval, sometimes savage – why even on a hot day the skies still hold threats of storm clouds ... '

There was more in the same vein, much more, words tumbling out like water splashing over stones in some endless waterfall. I was bemused, confused: could have listened forever, yet somehow felt strangely disturbed, aware of a distance between us.

When we were back in the cottage I tried to bridge this gap by asking her to show me some of her latest paintings. Perhaps I thought that as we looked upon them in unison we would be somehow mystically joined – in fact almost the opposite was true. As she pulled out one canvas after another and put it upon the easel for inspection so I was at once overwhelmed and filled with a sense of despair. Something about her work, perhaps her way of working – at any rate, the end result – represented an entry into a mysterious world which I knew I had not attained.

Perhaps at one time she divined what was going through my mind for she leaned forward, peering intently at one particular painting which showed the sea and land all intermingled, almost as if in consummation of each other.

'Strange – I can remember the day I did that in every detail. There had been a storm, and then it was all washed away and the sun came out, I went out and saw all this in a single glance and I knew I had to capture it – you know how it is, one just *knows*.'

She went on to describe how she came back and started painting. Somehow as she spoke the vision grew up before me not merely of the painting that was being created out of nothing upon a blank sheet of paper – but of the creator, too, this woman beside me, and how in the very act of creating she became curiously powerful and aware, her every limb moving in unison, the act a very physical thing ... and a very beautiful thing.

'Funny,' she said pensively. 'The sun and all that was a bit like today.'

She didn't look at me as she spoke and I knew that I still had not remotely reached her curiously private kingdom ... but that one day I must, or else I would surely die.

4

I entered then upon a strange, almost idyllic period of my life. Armed with my perpetual excuse of wishing to search through her paintings for potential illustrations to my stories I was able to pay regular visits to the lonely clifftop cottage near Land's End. Even though I am inclined in retrospect to imagine that she resented this intrusion upon her privacy I suppose at the same time like any artist she must have been flattered.

And of course there could be no doubting the genuineness of my admiration for her work. Almost every time I entered that magical white world of her studio I made some new discovery which managed, almost unbelievably, to outstrip the previous one. Sometimes, unable to restrain my wonder, I would gasp out my delight – hearing, Victoria might come over and stand beside me, looking at her own pictures as if for a moment through my eyes. On such occasions I would often notice a strange smile around her lips – a smile which illuminated her face so that it glowed in the same sensuality as her paintings.

At such moments I would often be overwhelmed by a strong physical urge for the woman beside me – an urge rendered all the more painful by the continued sense of her remoteness.

It was in vain that I tried to bridge the gap. Whenever I tried to talk to her at all intimately, as of her private life, she became wary.

'Oh, I'm not very sociable at all, you know. I lead a very solitary life … '

'But – you have friends – close friends?'

She shrugged.

'Some of the local fishermen. They take me out sometimes night fishing. I enjoy that.' That shrug again. 'It's natural. We're all Cornish … '

Somehow each piece of such information, far from helping me in any search, actively depressed me. Suddenly faced with this vision of her escaping into the shadowy night surrounded by her swarthy fishermen friends I found myself filled with an almost insane sort of jealousy, so that I could hardly bear to speak. Later, when sometimes I was to see Victoria among her fishermen friends, I was to realise that my instinct was perhaps not far wrong. There was an easy manner, a sort of abandonment about her movements and behaviour which was unmistakable – if only because so unusual. Many of the fishermen were young and bearded, vibrant with physical colours – they belonged decisively to their immediate environment, and so did Victoria. Together they seemed to merge together so that it seemed the most natural thing in the world for one of them to put his blue denimed arm around Victoria's shoulder, for another to run a teasing hand rufflingly through her dark hair. It was difficult for me to believe, then, that there were not other links between them, sensual and perhaps sexual. And so my jealousy grew and grew.

One day, overwhelmed, I ran out on to the cliffs above the cottage, finally slackening my pace and going to hide myself and my sorrows behind a huge granite boulder. From there I had a clear view of the cottage and curiosity compelled me to watch from afar.

After a while I was surprised to see Victoria emerge carrying not the usual sketch pad, but a brightly coloured towel. Intrigued I watched carefully and saw her take a path that seemed to lead almost over the edge of the cliffs. From there, I realised, she was setting off to follow a winding pathway that must lead right down to the seashore below.

After allowing time for her to get well on her way I ran silently across to the top of the cliff and looked cautiously over the side. I was just in time to see Victoria reach the bottom of the path where it ran out on to a small patch of golden sands – a beautiful remote spot, a beach of her own.

Even more intrigued I began making my way silently down the side, taking care to keep out of sight of the beach itself. In some ways I felt I was behaving despicably, like a peeping tom, yet I could not help myself. I wanted to know all about this woman: *everything*.

When I was within twenty feet or so of the beach I settled myself behind a rock and gazed down cautiously. I was just in time to see the sudden movement as Victoria came running from behind a rock where she had stripped off her clothes – now naked and indeed looking rather like some mermaid of old, she ran with flowing movements down to the edge of the sea. For a moment she stood poised there, holding her arms up as if in gratitude to the warm sun above – and then she had leaped into the water and with powerful strokes began swimming towards the nearby headland.

I watched for about half an hour that summer's afternoon as Victoria swam lazily about the small bay. At one time she climbed on to a distant rock and sunned herself, and though she was faraway I still had the same physically vivid impression of her body, as real and as vibrant as the granite rocks or the surging sea. Indeed that was the predominant experience of my watching her that day – a sense of herself, the woman, the painter, becoming inexplicably tangled with all those sensual paintings of the world around her – a feeling that somehow by her act of swimming she was merging with her very own material.

It was a strange sort of experience: as if in one sense I was inside her world – and yet, in another, remained as ever firmly outside.

Undoubtedly I found that afternoon's experience deeply unsettling. I can remember that day when I finally arrived home and went and sat in my little sitting room how almost unwillingly my eyes turned to look at the familiar paintings – and how in some way their usual familiarity seemed heightened – as if, as if indeed superimposed upon their shapes was another shape – the shape of their creator, brown and sinewy and fleshy, dripping with seawater.

The next time I went over to the cottage I tried hard to put these thoughts out of my mind and yet with Victoria standing at my side it was hard to do so. I was possessed with such a surge of physical longing that I found it hard to believe she could remain unaware. Perhaps she did indeed sense something, for I can remember she seemed at her most distant that day, answering me only in short syllables, obviously not pleased to see me at all.

Responding to this mood I tried vainly to plead my case.

'I hope you don't mind my coming like this ... but seeing your work, seeing you, it helps me to feel closer to understanding – Cornwall and all that.'

She shrugged.

'Perhaps.'

The strange thing was that the more I tried to enter her world, the less able I seemed to capture my own interpretation of Cornwall. My own writings seemed to dwindle. Day after day I would sit at my desk endeavouring to conjure up my usual images and metaphors – only to find my mind wandering, my eyes seeing not typewritten words but distant images, of twisting granite, of surging sea – above all, that naked body running down to meet the waves' embrace.

I was, I can now see, becoming besotted either by the woman or her work, it did not matter, the two were too intermingled ... either could be my damnation.

If I had been wise I would have stopped making these journeys across to that remote cottage. But we are not wise when in the grip of strange passions. And then again perhaps, to some extent after all she must by now have been aware of her effect upon me – perhaps, who knows, she could not resist occasionally dangling the bait. There must have been some kind of enjoyment in watching the victim suffer.

Or perhaps again, in some curious way, the experience helped to nurture her own work? Yes, I have often thought that – but, oh, the irony of it!

5

From time to time there were further art exhibitions at which Victoria's latest works would be shown. At such occasions I was kept at a distance: she might appear in company with fellow painters but she would hardly have more than a word for me. It was as if she was already regretting our brief contact – and yet something, perhaps merely vanity, made her unwilling to give up her undoubted hold upon me. And so in public I was ignored – in private I was still allowed to pay the occasional visit to the hallowed spot.

Once, just once, she actually came to visit me. At the time she made the excuse that she happened to be driving by but it may have been more deliberate than that, I don't know. I only know that one strange rather misty morning I heard the sound of a car engine drawing to a halt in the lane outside and then when I looked up there she was standing in the doorway, looking around with some curiosity at my private world which was yet so dominated by her paintings.

'How strange. I had quite forgotten some of these.'

She moved round, examining each of the paintings in turn.

'Each day they greet me like old friends,' I said diffidently. 'I am very fond of them.'

She laughed at that, the nearest to momentary affection I think I ever knew.

'Well, that's nice for you ... '

After that she seemed restless, and she did not stay very long. I had the curious feeling that she began regretting her visit almost as soon as she arrived. As if – as if even by the very gesture of making it she had broken some inner resolution. As soon as possible she made her departure: she never came again.

But I – I was unable to resist my pilgrimages. Like any drug addict I was drawn again and again, even though I knew there would be rebuffs and indifference.

It must have been about this period when Victoria began her new series of love paintings. I call them that, for they were indeed paintings of love – of a love affair with Cornwall. But somehow they went quite beyond the normal; indeed they could have been described as quite daring both in their scope and execution. Sometimes, looking back, I am sure that in a curious way she became possessed while executing those works. Once or twice I happened to be around her closely while she worked, and I am sure I detected about her movements, her approach, something close to desperation, an almost feverish behaviour – as that of someone afraid that if they did not hurry they might lose the essence of that for which they searched.

What Victoria searched for was a method of bringing Cornwall's magic and mystery alive. I could see in retrospect that she had been searching for this for years, there were obvious signs in her earlier works. Now, triumphantly, she had found an answer – now her landscapes, those great swirling splashes of shade and colour, of vivid lines and images – in some almost miraculous way they did become alive. And the way she achieved this, the very simple (and yet so difficult) way, was by transposing her vision of land and sea and sky into a physical image – into physical shapes and forms – into the bodies of man and of woman.

It was an extraordinary achievement, though of course to me a most disturbing one. What was so remarkable was that as soon as one saw the final painting, the decisive image – its rightness was obvious. Of course, of course! Of course the penetrating finger of a rocky promontory striking out bravely into the surging Atlantic waves – that was extremely physical, a sexual symbol. And again, the vast loneliness of a beach on a wintry day, or perhaps the stark outline of Zennor moors above the diminutive farmhouses and the distant sea – or more especially one of those towering carns rearing up into the sky – or again, even those originally man-made edifices of crumbling mine heads at Bottalack and Levant – now in the new paintings they were all cleverly refashioned and shaped into pronouncedly physical symbols, sometimes male, and sometimes female. The male images were usually associated with harsh cruel images of rock and stone and cliff ... the womanly images emerged more naturally, enveloping everything as if in some natural embrace.

Watching Victoria at work in those heady days I was struck again and again by the way in which she seemed literally to be consumed by this new passion. Sometimes I knew she worked for hours on end without stopping indeed as if unable to stop.

One day when diffidently, I had called over and found her bent as usual over her easel I ventured my query.

Why ... ?

She shrugged impatiently.

'It's been waiting for me I see that now. It was just a question of the right moment.'

'And when was that?'

She gave a strange, secretive smile.

'Oh, one night not long ago. Or rather – ' she paused, as if suddenly lost in some vivid memory ' – one morning. I woke up – and there it all was before me, as if a key had turned in a lock and everything was revealed.'

'Naked and unashamed?' I said before I could stop myself.

She did not turn her head, went on daubing at her painting: but around her lips, again played that secretive – and now, I understood, sensual smile.

'Yes, I suppose you could say that.' She daubed away effortlessly. 'Naked and unashamed … '

Somehow I knew at once, from that moment. Of course it is possible that I have misinterpreted the whole thing – yes, it is possible. But on that clear morning, seeing the look on her face, the smile at her lips, even hearing the faint mockery in her voice, I felt I knew for certain what lay behind the new outburst. After all what could be more logical? 'One night long ago … ' – Victoria, the woman, had fallen in love, perhaps with one of those dark-bearded fishermen, or perhaps someone else, some pale and romantic fellow painter – it did not really matter. What mattered was that from her own personal experience had spurted this vivid expression – indeed, as she said, a key had turned in the lock.

When I went away that day my mind, my whole being was in a turmoil. If I had the courage I would have interrupted Victoria at her easel, seized the familiar and secretly beloved body in my arms and made violent love to her. Perhaps that is what I should have done – even that I was meant to do? Who can ever know now?

But I lacked that courage. Instead I went away and fell to brooding, far away in my own lonely bungalow up on the moors. For days on end I stayed up there, hardly moving, standing in the middle of my little room and staring around, continually, at what I possessed of Victoria Amanda Hosking, half a dozen of those early paintings – recognising them as indeed early work and yet able to see in them all those vestiges of the later sexuality which was now emerging in full bloom.

Every now and then I found I could not bear to be in the same room as the paintings, and I would go and stride about the moors ... Yet sooner or later my feet would be impelled back towards the bungalow and I would enter, thirsty again to drink of the drug that was slowly consuming me, even if I did not realise.

Then one day something seemed to happen inside my brain. It was as if some protective shield which had been carefully placed in position suddenly gave way. To my confused mind it seemed as if the pictures themselves grew larger, to shine more brightly, even to move, ever so slightly. I had the startling image of them growing and growing so that eventually they would overwhelm not merely their surroundings, but the whole room – and myself with it, consuming me in a flurry of blood-red colours.

That was the day when, panic-stricken, I ran into the kitchen and picked up the large carving knife and ran back into the room. I stood for a long moment, wide eyed, looking around me at my advancing enemies – scornful and indolent, as coldly indifferent to my being as their creator. And then, courage bolstered up by fear, I leaped forward and began slashing at the canvases. Lost in some inner paroxsym of rage and frustration I leaped from one painting to another, cutting and slashing at each one ten and twenty times, until little was left of the canvas but bleeding torn strips ...

It was all over in a few minutes – yet in some ways they were the longest moments of my whole life. Even as I committed the act of execution I was dimly aware of all that it might purport. As someone once said every victory is also a defeat ... And even as I tore down the very last of the canvases, leaving it to join all the other bleeding areas, stumps of dying life on the floor around me, I could but acknowledge to myself that these were but six, that elsewhere in the world there existed dozens, perhaps hundreds, of other canvases. And that towering above them all, smiling her secret sensual smile, was their creator, even now inflamed with her new passions ...

6

Paradoxically from that moment when I destroyed those precious canvases I became aware of a, for the first time, sense of intimacy with Victoria. Although outwardly nothing had changed in our relationship, secretly I knew that it had: by my very act, even if it might be compared to a form of rape, I had undoubtedly come closer to the woman upon whom, I had to recognise, I now had a total fixation.

Perhaps encouraged by this illicit sense of satisfaction I decided upon further destruction. At the back of my mind, I think, the motives may have been confused. Was I seeking to destroy the paintings or the painter? Was I seeking to punish or perhaps, in a twisted way, to pay ultimate homage? It is a moot point ...

It did not concern me greatly as I went about my self-appointed task. All that mattered was to track down each painting, to take one last consuming look upon it – aware, deep in my secret being, that thus I would be last person on earth to have seen it, to have ravished it with my eyes – and then savagely and irrevocably, to destroy the flaming image.

I had to be careful, of course. And patient. But I soon found out where there were paintings – at galleries in Truro and Plymouth and Exeter – and I made journeys to each of these places and managed to commit my crime without being caught.

And then there were the galleries nearer at home, of course, at Newlyn and Penzance and here at St Ives. It was easier for me in such places where I was a familiar face and could wander around without anyone really noticing. Over a period, one week here, another week there, I managed to deface and destroy three large and striking canvases.

All this time, of course, there was quite a local outcry, and somewhat lurid tales in the press. Victoria herself was interviewed, indeed I saw her once on television. She looked pale and naturally rather distraught, but her attitude was basically scornful – no matter who was attacking her work, she said, no matter how many canvases were destroyed, she would paint more and more. The interviewer nodded sympathetically and at the same time commented pointedly that since that attacks began Victoria Amanda Hosking's paintings had soared in value.

In order to avoid any suspicion falling upon myself I had been careful to maintain my occasional visits to the cottage at Land's End. Each time I called there I commiserated unctuously with Victoria, so effectively indeed that one day she thanked me for being such a good friend. Instead of feeling ashamed of myself I felt the reverse, a curious sense of triumph. Surely, in some weird way, my aggression was paying? Wasn't I subtly more involved with Victoria than ever?

It was while standing in her studio that day that the final and obvious step occurred to me. All the paintings which had been destroyed so far were older work. The new work, the love paintings – the very material upon which all my jealousy was based, the revelation of Victoria's new sensuality – none of these had yet been shown publicly. They were all there in her studio, stacked in neat rows, waiting to be framed for an eventual and no doubt major exhibition.

I decided to destroy the whole lot, there in their secret home. I would have to wait, of course, but there would eventually come a time when I could be certain that Victoria was well out of the way, and then the way would be open for me to creep over and enter the cottage, to find the paintings and to destroy and destroy ...

Such an occasion was the next big opening over at the Penwith at St Ives. I knew that Victoria was definitely attending because she had mentioned so on my last visit, and this meant she would set off not later than seven o'clock for the twenty mile journey.

About an hour later, just when I reckoned that Victoria would be arriving in St Ives, I drove slowly along the lane leading to the cottage. I parked the car and climbed the steep path to the cottage. As I expected the front door was locked but when I went round to the back I found a kitchen window slightly ajar and managed to force it open and climb through.

Inside the cottage was strangely silent. I stood for a moment in the little hallway savouring the familiarity, imagining that I could catch a whiff of the odour of the woman who had but recently been present. At last I moved to the bottom of the staircase and began climbing up towards the big white studio ... feeling, as I went, for the jack knife in my pocket.

When I had entered the studio and closed the doors behind me I stood looking around, a little dazzled by the sudden blaze of colours. Victoria must have been sorting through her paintings and instead of being stacked away the canvases were spread about the room, hanging here and there, leaning against chairs and tables, creating an overwhelming sense of brightness and colour. It was almost too much to take in at a glance and I felt astonished yet again at the power and compulsion of these paintings. They seemed to glow and glisten with patent sensuality, the shapes and forms of the land and sea, the rocks and carns, became shadowy and evasive, twisting and turning before my very eyes – almost like human forms that were forever embracing.

I stared, bemused, at all this burning life around me, a little afraid, and yet in another way powerfully stimulated. It was as if slowly, secretly I was being drawn into the spell, as if perhaps some of this subterranean life was entering into me, too, so that I was becoming more vividly aware of everything around me.

I don't know how long I must have stood in that attitude, the knife in my hand half raised in the air, my eyes staring from one picture to another, the compulsion on me to destroy these tormentors, and yet some other emotion catching at me too. Perhaps I stood there for longer than I thought ... certainly I was lost to all other sounds. At last in a desperate attempt to break the impasse I lunged forward as if to strike at one of the paintings.

As I did so the voice came from behind me, startlingly; a familiar voice, but husky as with some strange emotion.

'So it was *you* all the time? – I thought perhaps it might be ... But why – ?'

I spun round. She was standing in the doorway, her face a strange mixture of surprise and anguish, and yet something more – something softer that might even have been compassion.

As if reading the expression in my own face she spoke simply.

'I had a premonition ... Someone so obsessed would be bound to seize the chance to come over when I was out of the way ... so I stayed behind.' She shrugged.

'And then of course I heard your car, so I went and hid in my bedroom, lay in the bed and waited. Then when I heard you creep up the stairs I became afraid, and so I followed you up here ... '

It is a little difficult now for me to remember what happened next. It seemed to me that I still had wild thoughts of raising my knife and cutting at the pictures ... and perhaps the awareness of this communicated itself to the woman standing a few feet away, like a shaft of illuminating light. Without speaking she moved slowly in my direction. As she did so her hands came up and she held them out towards me. But strangely it was not so much a gesture of supplication, rather something quite different – a suggestion of caring, of protectiveness.

'You know you don't want to really ... do you?' she whispered at last.

She came closer and closer: I became aware of her dark eyes burning brightly into my own – had the sensation of her seeing into my very soul.

'Is it the paintings? Is that what troubles you? Is there something about the paintings ... ?'

She hesitated, and then coming right up to me startled me by raising one hand and putting it gently on my brow, brushing my hair back in a soothing movement.

'The paintings are me,' she said huskily. 'If you destroy the paintings you are destroying me. Do you hate me all that much? No, of course I can't believe it. No you don't, do you?'

With a curiously decisive gesture she put her other arm forward and round my shoulder and slowly drew me into her embrace. As she did so the open knife in my hand brushed against her bare arm and I was conscious of the blade against her flesh. Quickly, in horror, I let it fall to the ground.

There was a faint spot of blood where the skin had been slightly punctured, but she shook her head as I looked at it unhappily.

'No matter,' she whispered. 'No matter … '

All around me I was conscious of the paintings, gathering as if in a silent army in their blaze of familiar sensuality, their secret power radiating – just as now, all at once, I could feel the same secret power emanating from the body that was all enveloping me even more closely than the paintings. I had the curious sensation as if I had gone wandering over wild moors and suddenly come upon some hidden place, a granite and secret kingdom.

'Stop worrying,' she whispered. 'You don't have to hate any more, you don't have to be afraid, you don't have to feel shut away. Because, see, *I* am here … '

Somehow I was conscious of her moving away for a moment, away to the couch in the corner of the room, sinking down upon it in a languorous movement … and as she did so, very deliberately, I saw that she was unbuttoning the green blouse she wore, unbuttoning it and opening it out as she lay back upon the couch … Watching, bemused, I had the sensation of looking upon one of her paintings, the landscape and the seascape merging into a single white, white figure, the breasts suddenly bared and exposed to the sunshine in the sky … and I realised that she was beckoning to me, beckoning to me urgently.

'Come over here,' she whispered. 'There's no need to kill and destroy … there are other ways … '

The rest is lost in total confusion. Somehow I clawed my way over to the couch and there hardly daring to breathe, I took her in my arms, feeling for the first time that burning flesh which I had so long desired. How she had guessed at this solution, this ultimate answer, I will never really know. Some instinct, I suppose, perhaps even the instinct of self-preservation – the preservation of her self that was forever bound up with those paintings. She knew that they must not die and if to save them she had to give herself to a stranger, well that was a small price to pay.

Besides, somewhere deep down, no doubt, there must have been yet another layer of sensuality which could but savour the experience ... As, more and more aroused, I became more positive in my own movement, holding her so tightly that she gasped out of pain and pleasure, so her own physical reactions became more inbued with passion – and so imperceptibly at first then with growing fire and even anguish, our love-making began, kissing with bruising lips, biting at warm flesh, stroking limbs that grew fury to touch ...

At some stage we slid slowly from the couch on to the studio floor and there at last, surrounded on all horizons by those same wondrous paintings, their own fires rising to the ceiling – at last, miraculously, something happened that I had never dared imagine and briefly and triumphantly I captured and possessed the body (if not the soul) of Victoria Amanda Hosking, white upon white, limbs entwined with limbs, a rising crescendo of urgency, until all passion was spent ...

7

I wish, like in all the best fairy tales, I could go on to describe how after that evening Victoria and I joined together eternally, how we married and lived happily ever after, painting our pictures and writing our books.

It was not like that at all. When I wrote that all passion was spent that was literally the fact of the matter. Perhaps, indeed I am almost certain, as a woman Victoria was much wiser and subtler than a mere man. After all she was fighting for more than her chastity or even her life – but for her art, which was even more important. She must have recognised that in some twisted way I had come to confuse her body with her paintings, and indeed it is more than probable that when she stayed behind that night she had already the plan formulated in her head to end this confusion once and for all.

At any rate, that was what happened. For a long time after

our lovemaking we lay in peace on the big white carpet, replete
and consummated. When at last I opened my own eyes I
looked sideways and saw that Victoria's were still closed. There
was upon her face a strange look, as of contentment, and this
was perhaps my only, yet most valuable reward. I knew in that
moment that in some part of her subconscious I would always
have a place, if only because of the extraordinary and tortured
part I had played in her life.

But I knew, too, that this was the end of it. I recognised that
no matter how I struggled, I could never enter into the soul of
Cornwall as she had done. She was part of it, as naturally as
lichen on the granite – I must remain outside, a superficial
observer.

Carefully I rose from the floor, leaving Victoria still
sleeping. For a brief moment I looked quickly around the
room at all those familiar sights – ah, but I would never forget
them, never, never!

Then, careful to make no sound I crept to the door and
down the staircase, and out into the lane, heading for my car.
It was nearly dusk now and the sun was setting on the horizon,
illuminating magically the distant humps of the fabled Scilly
Isles. All around there was the smell of heather and the hum of
insects ... and far below the restless sound of the surging sea. It
was a magical world that would have made a marvellous
subject for yet another painting ...

I got into my car, started the engine, and drove back across
the moors to my distant home. When I got there I started
packing at once, and then when all was done I lay down for a
brief sleep. As soon as it was dawn, I packed everything into
the car, and drove away – out of St Ives, out of Cornwall, out
of the West Country altogether.

I live now many hundreds of miles away, in the placid
flatness of an eastern county. I am still writing, still moderately
successful, though I suppose I have learned my limitations.
One of them is that every now and then I may read some item
in one of the cultural weeklies, about a new exhibition by
Victoria Amanda Hosking, and how successful a painter she

has become. I am always glad to know about the success, but there it ends. I fold up the magazine and put it away and get on with my ordinary life. It seems better that way.

II

Gone to the Wars

The soldier marched his first gleam-shafted bayonet down the familiar street and out to the dust-worn plains, away from the sweet tears of the gutters.

The pebble that once stirred the hopeful womb was imprinted into an astronomical number. The baby's eyes were rounded into cold steel bullets, the first toothless laugh was the grim white line of a desert-face, the fresh fair skin was stained a bitter brown by the killer's sun. Off to the wars marched the tricycle child and the satchelled hero-worshipper, the street-corner idler and the family joker, the time-born event-fated wearer of the sullen brown greatcoat and the leather sweat-boot; the last man in the fourth row of the swinging battalion. He was two paces from the dust-gathering boots of the rear line and two paces from the disinterested freedom of the low brambled hedges.

The afternoon air rang with the clipped clop of old boots and new boots, the steady tom-tom of dancing war bloods. Now in the wide wandering bareness the beginning was a bright brown drummer and an isolated piper. Now in the forlorn far horizon the end was a thoughtful old sergeant and a tired mule. Now in the isolated aridness the middle was a fat-bellied snake of three hundred, three-lined mocking bayonets.

Now in the endless war march the soldier looked at the grunting convoy of petrol devils and remembered the King Harry charges and the Arab horses that pawed the ground in olden years. He eyed the emotionless wireless turrets of the oven-raised cars and remembered the joyful colours of a hundred waving flags and the old dreams of a dash of glory. He stared thoughtfully at the wicked long field gun with the shining snout and remembered the broken lances of a thousand quixotic white knights. He saw the malicious tommy-gun and the were-wolf grenade carrier and the drab gas container and the spitting green metals; the darkened, heavy air shone with his vague memories of a clean white sword and the chivalrous shield, and he glanced more warmly at the single fresh shortness of his clean-bladed bayonet.

The way lay across the plain of the unprotective dust, but the soldier walked along in the sheltering dream of a faraway mind. The soldier's brown boots crunched over ragged pathways, but his mind floated smoothly through a cloudless sky.

When I was a small boy we used to play soldiers around an old sand heap, he remembered surprisedly. There were eight of us and we used to take sides and be generals and field-marshals and colonels and captains; we were never just soldiers, he remembered wistfully. Some of us used to stand on top of the sand heap and defend it to the death and some of us used to stand back and then charge up the sand heap like the cavalry, he remembered quite clearly. We used to fight with wooden swords and paper pellets and water pistols in those days, he remembered happily. (I remember the day when I threw a flour bomb from behind a tree and hit the ginger-haired boy on his head.)

We got tired of it in the end, it began to seem rather silly like all our games, and then we used to walk about the village and go to the pictures and do homework, he remembered thoughtfully. Now I am a real soldier marching off to a real war, thought the soldier, unreally, an odd cold compartment opening in some distant corner of his antique head.

Away on the destined horizon blew the curling smoke from a hundred hidden flames; the spat metal hissed and rained on some lonely land; the long-rumbled rolls tumbled through the haze. Listening, the soldier lost the safety of an artificial memory. His eyes riveted into their steely sockets and glared down the long road and watched, relieved, the friendly waves of the returning juggerwheels with their masturbating guntips. He marched on, marching his fifth mile and his fortieth furlong and his eight thousandth and eight hundredth yard and his twenty-six thousandth and four hundredth foot. Then he began to notice the whining whippet cars, with their wounded dents and their scarred sides and the white looks in their eyes.

The soldier looked away and hummed a pointless refrain, the three hundred soldiers looked away and hummed their pointless refrains; their voices suddenly swelled into the air and drowned the distant night-music. 'There's a sweet, sweet girl in my old home town,' sang the marching soldiers. 'And she's waiting there for me,' echoed the solitary soldier in his guttural helmet. His eyes peered caressingly about the innumerable backs and felt the unexpected warm friendship of them. The soldier sang louder and wilder, at the top of his voice, and was in tune with their tune and in step with their steps, and they sheltered one another's wondering minds with their warm humanity.

Then the skies opened and the first bumble bee screamed into the lives and deaths of the back-street boys. The soldier paralysed in his dust tracks, hearing the death-whistle past his neck, seeing a stout man scream and writhe in his steps. The soldier choked in his fear gasps, watching the snake wriggle and burst open, the river of blood drowning the familiar dust. The soldier trembled on the hard, parched ground and felt earthquakes shake the world.

Ten lifetimes fled in a last minute. Now I am a real soldier, thought the soldier in his hoped-for escape. The bumble bees flew away on a happy trial, blaring their triumph.

The soldier stood up and breathed the fresh, free air, among the groaning gargoyles. The prayed-for only son stood unhurt among the blue bleedings, watching the slow life trickling out of the side-mouth of a twitching corpse. The farewelled hero screamed inside his stomach, discovering the open entrails of an old campaigner and the dead smile of a girl's sweetheart. The brass-stamped digit winced a personal horror and an individual terror, following the bullet into the spewn-out eye of a fair-haired boy. Somewhere a severed arm lay pointing along the dusty road.

March! March! March! wheedled a frightened bully brigadier. March! March! March! pleaded a nervous living subaltern. March you devils, march! yelled a petrified sergeant. March, march, march, march, march, march, mumbled the dull-eyed men, the dull-eyed two hundred living bayonets.

March! cried the soldier to his own small heart, and he squared his drooped shoulders and stepped into the straggled column. He marched steadily along the winding road of the side-strewn lorries, away from the unbelievable afternoon and the labouring medicals. He gazed straight ahead of him, under his weary thick helmet, and saw only the thinned blur of the swaying necks, the strange lop ears and the red, red bandages.

Five miles to the front whispered the rumour wind. Four miles to the front whispered the rumour wind. Three miles to the front whispered the rumour wind. There is no front said a grave-eyed man at an office desk, plotting his abstract maps.

Two miles to the front whispered the fearful rumour wind. A sudden bomb burst in the lowering clouds, scattering the wild steel lumps on to tinkling helmets, and a man and a man and a man reeled into deadness. There is no front said a stout jovial man at an evening conference, in the padded club armchair.

One mile to the front whispered the terrified wind. The whistle of five shells screamed low in the air and frenzied the wagon horse into a fit. There is no front, said the waistcoat-thumbing politician on his happy platform.

Halt! yelled the stumbling officer, through his bloody lips, and they stood silently on the edge of downward fields, in the amazing dusk. There is no front, said the discerning military critic in the big city press room.

Dig! yelled the faltering officer with the heavy eyelids, and the two hundred shiny new boys began to create the cold out-post trench with its oozing water. Dig! Dig! Dig! yelled the hoarse-husked officer and the sensitive subaltern and the swearing sergeant. There is no front, there is no front, there is no front chanted honey-sweet voices in the pleasure parks and the forest-ringed cities.

Dig, dig, dig, dig, dig! echoed the resounding mind of the soldier, the time-worn soldier from the lost village and the sweet memories. Dig! he thought in his sweated half-nakedness, until the mounded earth was a cloak to half the sky, and he stood in a corner of the uprooted soil, blinding his streaked eyes to the mad night's flashes, drumming his ears into the ground at the near whistles of the death spears.

A big flame seared the sky like an old wound. Mother of God! screamed the soldier. A wild howl rent the air. Oh, Holy Mary! prayed the frozen-bowelled soldier. A mad wind blew away the air and cleft open the six hours' digging into a pulped vegetable plant. Lord in Heaven! whispered the soldier, lying in an isolated cornpatch, the squelching mud thrown around him and the moaning music a dirge of the night.

God give me strength! muttered the ordinary soldier with the back-garden memory, plunging into the red welter with his humane help. God give me strength! said the old-eyed soldier with the fogged mind, in the cold sweated dawn ... Out of the vast crater, out of the smoking wound, crawled the dull red men, the last hundred bayonet carriers with the tattered tunics and the wild, wild eyes.

Now I am a real soldier, thought the empty-headed soldier in the frightened morning sun. He giggled. Now I am a real soldier, thought the raw-bellied soldier in the open air breakfast field. He laughed tears. (Now I am a real soldier and my folks will be proud of me and my girl will love me and the village flags will wave in my honour and I will be quite a hero when I go on leave thought the day-old soldier, in the heat of the hell-field.)

The bayonets gleamed in the sun as they lay grimly in the startled grass. The soldier lay silent and thoughtful, sweat and soil interlining his face. The soldier crouched in the long stalks with a grim rifle pointing to the enemy forests. The soldier murmured a text-book phrase and desperately remembered the loud brass bands. The soldier fingered the cold steel skin of his rifle and felt the blood washing cold in his expectant veins. Forward! uttered the tired officer with the eye of no hope and the blank mind of the past or future.

They crawled slowly through the long grass in the steady

rhythmic sound of the jungle-beaters. They crept down the long field, down the gladed valley to the menacing woods that lay in the hollows. Their stomachs rolled over tiny stones and crumpled soils, crushing the young stalks. Their eyes stared into the firm brown ground and wept wearily. They crawled along a hedge and across a lane and warily scattered towards the soft green approach of the doom wood.

The soldier thought of his last leave in the merry village, the laughter of the wine. He saw himself in the proud mirror, he thought of the swanking dance and the seductive moonlit walk. His mind's eye paced down the main street and round the chemist's corner and up the laburnum grove to the red-tiled house with the friendly winking moonlight, the brown-berried girl in the deep-dreamed bedroom.

The soldier crawled in a no-man's field and remembered a soft skin and a gentle-curved breast; but a cold, stuttered machine-gun jaggedly poured molten metal into yearning bodies, in the senseless sunshine.

The soldier crouched in the field of peaceful harvest corn and remembered a last night's sleep in the cool bedclothes; but a savage iron hand sprayed rains of death over the screaming boys, like a farmer's happy mowing machine.

(I am alive … alive, alive, alive, alive … thought the flat-faced soldier in the indigo hay. Alive, alive, alive, alive, thought the charmed minds of ten bright guardsmen, leaning over their immortal precipices and swaying in the wind.)

Forward! cried the incredible officer, leaping into the animal open and hurling his madness into the sadistic wood-world. Forward! cried the mesmerised ghosts of the fields, with the disappearing bowels and the frozen hearts and the bloodless veins and the buried emotions and the blind eyes and the mechanical minds, springing giant-like into the huge sky horizon and flinging their careless limbs through the hailing bulletstorm and the flooding red metal and the vicious stutter, up to the belching mouth of the quaking gun's nest.

War! blared the thick headlines of the comfortable newspapers.

War! delcared the brass-peaked commander in the exciting headquarters.

War! exclaimed the laconic gunner with the string trigger to a mile-a-second whistle.

War! grinned the beret-capped driver of a melting molten tank, with the armour plates ...

War! War! War! screamed the soldier in the exultant frenzy of his nine-inch steel power, throwing his wild point straight into the soft, surprised bowels.

War! screamed the ten death-masks, and they smothered the crunched bees in their molten nest and stamped the blood and the flesh into the pulp of their broken bones until the sun stuttered into an ungainly silence.

Hours and hours and days and days and weeks and weeks and months and months and years and years and centuries and centuries later he stood laughing against a tree. The world lay upside down before him, in a tortured cesspool, and the other soldiers were gone into the mists of madness. He was alone.

Comrade! hailed the soldier.

Comrade! hailed the sudden lonely soldier.

Comrade! cried the soldier, in the quiet forest with the morning hiss of death in the dewy tree roots.

Comrade! whispered the ground ... and the soldier leapt to the side of a torn red tunic and the begging eyes of a morning machine gunner. (Comrade, comrade, comrade! thought the hate-ebbed soldier as he stemmed the thick life stream and pitied the slim boy from the unseen horizon.)

The soldier hooked the baby arms around his neck, took the sadwitted body on his curved shoulders, straightened up with the deadweight devil of another world on his clinging back and the soft sweet whisper of twisted humanity in his ear. He slowly dragged himself across the shattered wood and out into the false sunshine and down the long field again. He whispered consoling whispers to the dying head on a lolling shoulder, and bathed the bright eyes of himself in a mirror, and smiled the faint tremulous smile of the little boy in some playtime cherry orchard.

Now I am a real soldier thought the soldier in the empty-hearted land, sobbing under the glory-gored sky.

He staggered on across the fields and the woods and the lanes and there was no grass and no leaves and no human breath in the long swirling dust, only the vast loneliness of the heart ... only the old, sad eyes of the soldier. His memories in a dead field and his enemy on his back and his toy rifle dragging on the dry gloomy stones.

III

The Stepfather

When the girl was eight years old he used to bathe her in a huge galvanised bath, before a roaring fire in the kitchen. At first the mother did this, as many other tasks, but after a while the stepfather suggested that he should take on some of the responsibilities. And, pleased at his interest, the mother had agreed. She would sit back in the armchair, rocking herself slightly, watching with pleasure as the big, rather plump man treated her daughter with such gentleness, with such tender and kind movements. There were not many men, she told herself, who would have so completely accepted into their lives not merely a woman, but her child by another man.

But it was not as simple as that. When he had first met with the mother, it had been with no thought of her broken marriage, of her child. He had seen her at a dance, a woman of thick rather sensuous limbs, wearing a low cut dress that showed much of her breast, and with her dark hair puffed out in strange defiance – as if, her pouting lips emphasized, she challenged any man to take her. He had been wanting a woman for a long time: automatically he gravitated into her life. She was glad to find a haven of safety again, she did not want to face all the turbulence through which she had just passed. Though she doubted if she could ever again love anyone, she found a certain satisfaction in this man's ardour, and she knew she could grow fond of him. He for his part found the physical contact, the sheer experience of passion, satisfying enough in itself. He did not trouble much to consider whether they were in love.

In the same way, he had not really considered the child. If he had done so, he might have drawn a barrier, insisted that there should be a new life, just the two of them, the child left with grandparents. But just at the time when he might have thought on those lines he had been diverted by a small incident. It was only the second occasion he had met the child. The three of them had been sitting by a lake in the park, one hot May afternoon. The child was playing by the water, pushing out little wooden sticks as imaginary boats. For a time the mother had had to go away, a call of nature. In just those few moments there was a splash and a wail. Looking up he saw the little girl floundering in the lake. She wasn't in danger, of course, but she was wet and frightened. Dashing forward he picked her up and carried her over to the grass. Her clothes were soaking wet, and she was shivering. Doing what seemed the best thing, he took off her clothes, opened his coat and huddled the child close against his chest.

It was then that he became physically aware of her. Without really thinking, he allowed his hand to wander over the small body, feeling the miniature woman's shape, the firm thighs, the rounded buttocks, the slender legs – and the surge of flesh rising upwards, to the tiny shoulders, the neck, the pink ears. Yet it was not this alone, either; but just at that moment he saw the mother coming back across the grass, walking with the slightly feline, familiar movements which had first aroused him, her legs flashing white and provocative in the sunlight.

'Why,' he whispered to himself, 'I suppose you'll be another like your mother.'

Another, he thought secretly, another with thick limbs and sensual lines, another throbbing with blood and heat and life. And thinking like that he held the child tight and tighter, until she began to cry.

After that it seemed natural enough to keep the child. She was younger then, of course, less of a personality. But now, at eight, now that she was more established, he found her strange, secret attraction even more pronounced. It was as if – but no, he could not really put it into words, it was just something of which he was aware. He could tell it to no one, least of all to the mother. He could only think about it, secretly, to himself: and seek, subtly, the moments of contact; as now when he gave the little girl her weekly bath, taking the soap between his hands and then rubbing the froth steadily, rhythmically over her pert, yet shapely young body.

In those days nothing was said directly, nothing admitted, between the stepfather and the girl. It was all a matter of touch, perhaps of imagination – certainly of intent rather than fulfilment – something of which he was rather nervously conscious, of which he was hardly aware. The mother, watching placidly, thought about them sentimentally, what a sweet picture they made, the big man playing on the sands with the little girl, or carrying her piggy-back up the stairs – or sitting at her bedside, reading a story before tucking her in for the night. It in no way disturbed her that her daughter sought increasingly the man's company, for in the mother's eye, by a process of automatic adjustment, he had become the girl's father – and as such the relationship was simple and uncomplicated and pure. She wished only that she could now have another child by this man himself, so that he would know the even greater pleasure of being father to his own flesh.

By chance, this never occurred. It was a factor that did not trouble the stepfather, for he was increasingly absorbed in his stepdaughter. Another child would to him have been too great a diversion. To the mother it was a sadness without being a heartache: regrets were compensated by the beauty of her husband's love for his stepdaughter. That love obviously grew and increased – and, she was pleased to observe, obtained its just reward in the return of the girl's affection. Of that there could be no doubt.

The stepfather discovered this in a hundred sweet ways. By the way the girl clung to him, by the words she whispered, by the things she wrote, by the way she looked at him when he came into a room. And the knowledge was a powerful fuel to his desire, was added incentive to his ambition. Now that he knew he held power, he wielded it without thought.

She was ten by now, slender and delicate, yet with the first flowering of her youth. She had soft, rosy cheeks, and a high clear forehead, and her hair, dark and long like her mother's, was still in pigtails. She was pretty in a forlorn sort of way; but her real attraction, already, was like her mother's – in the lines of her body, in the curve of her limbs, in the way of her walk.

This the stepfather was aware of in a curiously intense manner, out of proportion to reality. For every time he looked at the girl he saw her mother as well; and the slender thing that walked down the road towards him was a woman as well as a girl.

And now, knowing his power, he demanded from the girl impulses beyond her immediate understanding, yet which, fearful of losing this powerful affection, she forced herself to give.

'How about a kiss for your father?' the man would say jovially, lifting her on to his knee. And the girl lifted her face dutifully, but not entirely with pleasure; for experience taught her to expect not the comforting, motherly kiss of her mother, but a strange and disturbing kiss, in which the man's lips were thick and parted, and strangely hot, and the teeth pressed into her flesh painfully. It was a kiss that to her was meaningless, and yet which she could not forget, and never would.

And so when the man, said, on other occasions, 'Look out, I'm going to tickle a certain little girl,' the girl's attempt at escape was half real – for even as a part of her wanted to be tickled, wanted the attention, another secretly dreaded the moment of contact, when the stranger's hands wandered about her body, searching and probing, awakening disturbing reactions that should have slumbered longer. While on the surface the girl remained innocent about the meaning of these furtive embraces, the deeper, more secret knowledge that bred within her recognised them for what they were – and, secretly accepted them.

So, as the girl grew older, she did so on two levels. On the one she was the girl at school, in her tunics and gym dresses, among her friends, carrying her school books, absorbed in the strange unfoldment of the normal world around her. On the other she led a secret life, encompassed by herself and her stepfather. It was a world into which she seemed to descend, step by step, as into a pit, aware that the journey back would be more difficult with each step – yet enticed onward by the secret knowledge, the secret power, the secret of one so close so trusted.

For some years, the stepfather was delighted, endlessly excited by this new avenue of his life. He watched his stepdaughter's blossoming out into a pretty young girl with a more than paternal eye, savouring each bloom of prettiness, each flash of new and youthful beauty. How fresh, how lovely, how delicately beautiful was the girl he thought – and he touched her pretty hair, her thoughtful face, her rounded limbs. And at each touch the girl's pleasure secretly increased, her innocence faded.

But just as the girl approached full bloom, the bud unfolding into womanhood – just as the stepfather eagerly saw a passionate end to his long and secret wooing – so an unexpected change entered their relationship. For the stepfather had educated the young girl not wisely but too well. He had matured her in haste – now she left him to repent at leisure. In brief, the young girl, abruptly and vividly made sexually aware of men, looked around her and found them everywhere; and far younger and more attractive, more handsome and dashing, than her stepfather.

It was then, too late, that the stepfather realized what he had made of his stepdaughter. She was seventeen, rich and warm and lovely with the flame of her youth. She had a strong face like her mother's, a sensual beauty of line like her mother's – and a hot blooded passion such as had died in her mother. All this might have slumbered awhile, to seep out gradually with the years, along the slow and respectable pathway of engagement and marriage and family life. But the stepfather had altered all this: he had installed into the girl a secret knowledge, of caresses, of embraces, of men's desires, of women's desires. Thus equipped, the girl embarked on a long and exquisite voyage of discovery, savouring the delights and exotic excitements of many men's ardours other than her stepfather's.

Her mother could not understand it. 'What has come over the girl? We brought her up so well. We gave her love and security ... You were like a real father to her. And now look at her – she behaves like a harlot.' And often she wept on her husband's shoulder, while he patted her exasperatedly on the back.

His anguish, of course, was even greater. He could never believe, never accept the reality of the situation. He was forever waylaying his step-daughter. 'How can you do this to me? I have given you so much!' And he would stare beseechingly into her eyes, clasping her soft young hands in his hardening older ones. 'You are cruel and unkind. I cannot bear to think of you with all these men.' And sometimes such was his agitation, he would even go down on his knee in supplication before this exquisite vision of loveliness, roses in her cheeks, starlight in her eyes, her body curving gracefully in the repose of a woman awakened.

But the girl remained unmoved. She had a long memory. She was no fool, not now. She appreciated, even though she knew it was too late to undo, the possible harm that her stepfather had done to her. And so she was merciless in her revenge.

'That's right, stepfather, down on your knees. Cringe – well you might do. It's true as you say, I owe you much – much that I can never repay. You have taught me the wickedness of innocence, the excitement of experiment, the beauty of lust. How can I ever thank you enough? It's difficult, but I will try – by following your teaching, benefiting from your advice, acting on your precepts.'

Then she would laugh into his face, and carry her glittering beauty off for another man to savour.

Oh, thought the stepfather, that I should live to endure such shame, such humiliation! And gradually he lost all his zest and sparkle, all his verve and dash, so that even his ageing wife was inspired to comment: 'My dear you are looking so tired, so ill – so *old*.' And indeed, he knew the comment to be a just one, though he laughed it off with a flicker of bravado.

Then, in order to preserve his sanity, the stepfather immersed himself in other things; in his work, in his garden, in books and paintings and other intellectual pursuits, in a somewhat overdue but quite genuine tenderness towards the welfare of his wife. It was many years since he had thought so much about her, but now that she was old, and rather poor in health, he turned to her with sudden gratitude, remembering her as he had first seen her, glistening sweetly on the dance floor. In this welcome surge of real affection, he gave himself and his mind to his wife, bringing to her last years a very deep and real happiness; so that when she died, rather early in her life, her existence did not seem to have been empty or without purpose, but indeed one for which she was profoundly grateful.

At the time of his wife's death it seemed to the stepfather that his own life might be considered closed, though he was still only in his early fifties. Upon reflection he felt he had lived a worthy enough life: he had worked hard, he had married, and though he had not procreated, he had at least made his wife happy. Only one thing blemished the picture, rankling in his mind – somehow he felt, he had failed badly in the case of his stepdaughter. He had embarked on a project of some grandeur of conception, and made a miserable mess of things. This knowledge depressed and embittered him, but as he believed he had long ago given up all earthly vanities and ambitions and now resigned himself to the placidity of his remaining years.

But one day, as typical of the wayward circumstances of life, there came a knock at the door of his house. On opening it he found his stepdaughter standing there, with a suitcase in one hand, and a look of appeal in her eyes.

'Why,' said the stepfather, uncertainly. 'What do you want?' His stepdaughter came in and closed the door pointedly behind her.

'If you don't mind, I'd like to come back here to live. I could have my old room, couldn't I? And I won't be in the way – I –'

Then she burst into a flood of tears which rendered all further conversation both impossible and unnecessary. 'Poor girl,' thought the stepfather. 'Some unhappy love affair, some stupid quarrel.' And quite without thinking, he comforted the girl in his most fatherly fashion, soothing her troubled head on his breast, patting her shoulders comfortingly and generally attempting to relieve her misery. 'Don't you worry,' he said. 'It will all work out all right. You'll patch thing up, don't worry. I'm sure he really loves you, whoever he is.'

That night the stepfather made a meal for the unexpected guest, and afterwards put a hot water bottle in her bed and saw that she was tucked in and off to sleep by ten o'clock. 'A good night's rest will do you the world of good. In the morning we'll see what can be done.'

But in the morning somehow, she gave him little chance to get around to patching up whatever had upset her. Somehow, without his being able to do much about it, his stepdaughter made herself immediately at home, taking charge of the kitchen, seeing to the ordering of food, producing a most enjoyable meal.

'But really,' he protested at the end of it. 'This is no life for you. What about – what about your other life?'

The girl looked at him carefully. Strictly speaking, of course, she was no longer a girl, but a woman in her thirties, shapely, strongly built, an air of maturity adding something faintly exciting to her obvious charms. Since the time she had left home she had pursued her way through two marriages and innumerable affairs of varying duration. She had experienced almost every form of love-making from the passionate to the poetic, from the ardent to the arduous, from the physical through the mental to the spiritual. And she was bored with the lot.

'I have no other life,' she said simply, and began to clear away the lunch things.

The stepfather did not quite know what to make of the position. Since his wife's death he had settled down to a form of bachelor existence which had proved very satisfying. He was old enough to have formed habits of regularity, of procedure, which gave life a certain flavour of enjoyment which a younger person could not have understood. These now went by the board. His stepdaughter forced him to come for long walks in the parks, or to accompany her to art shows and theatres, sometimes even on a day's outing to the country – outings which at first he undertook under protest, only to find himself enjoying them. Striding along country lanes in his tweed suits, beside the shapely form of a young and attractive woman, he found himself recovering quite a bit of his old zest for life.

In the evening they would sit by the fire reading, or listening to the wireless, a period of peace, of sensual quiet. Often the stepfather would look across at the bent head of his stepdaughter and wonder if surely it wasn't his wife sitting there.

And one evening when he was looking across and thinking like that the woman looked up and met his eyes. Without a word being spoken she jumped to her feet and crossed over and sat herself close to her stepfather on the couch. At the same moment that he felt her warm body pressed against his, a shock that was at once delightful and familiar, he saw her face upturned to his, her lips open, hot air exuding from them and enveloping his own breath and thoughts.

'Kiss me!' she said urgently, insistently: a command that brooked no refusal.

The stepfather could never remember a kiss like that before, and neither for that matter could his stepdaughter. It was like a first kiss and yet a last one; a promise and yet somehow a fulfilment. It defied analysis, for it was quite irrational: yet it was pregnant with significance, for it set a seal on their life together. It had no beginning and no end: or rather it had begun when the stepfather had first set eyes on the small girl romping in a park, and it would end only when his eyes were closed forever.

The woman knew that. She had known it really all the time: as the child romping, as the schoolgirl half disgusted and half intrigued, as the young woman evil and sadistic in her revenge, as the woman of the world voyaging upon far seas – through all her journeys this secret knowledge had remained within her. A man had shaped her feminine life, that man must end her feminine life. So she had to come back. It was the last remaining excitement, the only discovery yet to be made.

They were blissfully happy. Everything they did was twice as satisfying as it might have been: for they lived and breathed in a world of their own making, with a secret history known to them only, and a fulfilment possible to them only. The stepfather reaped a late harvest from the seeds he had planted so early. His stepdaughter achieved in their union some sort of penance for all her lost innocence: it was as if she was born again and she was as pure and perfect as a young bride.

The stepfather never quite knew what to make of things. He did not feel he had really deserved such happiness. But, being a wise man, he accepted it for the delightful thing it was. There would be time enough, he reflected, for him to consider the profound implications of the whole affair when he was too old to consummate it any further.

IV

The Machines

Up among the hills of Penwith, although it's at the far end of Cornwall, there are cottages and farms, and even whole villages where you could live all your life without a sight of the sea – yes, and that despite the fact that the sea stretches everywhere a matter of six or seven miles away. The villages cluster into little hollows and the folds of the bare moorland hills rise all around, almost as if in protection.

Protection from what? Well, from the terrible winds that sweep in from the Atlantic, a good many folk would say. But there are other, even more terrible things against which the encircling hills might offer their shelter. The sea itself, for instance – I met a man once in one of the tiny Penwith villages who admitted quite frankly that he felt more at ease, happier indeed, because in such a remote and sheltered spot he was hidden from the sea. No, he wasn't a seaman or anything like that. But he'd had a peculiarly intimate relationship with water, I gathered that. And there were memories, unforgettable memories which somehow, I sensed, couldn't be hidden from even behind our gaunt Cornish hills.

Mind you, Howells – that was the man's name, Welsh, of course, so naturally he felt quite at home in a Celtic land like Cornwall – well, Howells had come far enough in his attempts to escape from his memories. Three hundred miles or so, in fact. And still you could see in his eyes, stolid and comfortable-looking old man that he was, some flickering vision of a disturbing past.

I suppose I became rather intrigued. I was living in Penzance at the time, but often I would catch a bus out to the cross-road, and walk half-a-mile or so down the winding valley road into the village, and up to the little pub called The Engine Inn. Rather ironical, I thought afterwards, that old Howells should spend his last drinking days in a pub of that name.

We got talking over a glass of beer one day, and then we often used to have a little chat. We became quite friendly, in fact, so I suppose it was only natural that we should finally start rummaging into the past. I was always a bit curious to know just why a man like Howells, quite a town-bird in his way, should choose to retire to such a remote spot. I think we got around to the real heart of the matter on one occasion when I invited him to come out with me on one of the Newlyn pilchard fishing boats, belonging to a pal of mine. Old Howells lifted up his sharp little head – rather like a bird's it was – and looked quite horrified. No, he wouldn't hear of it. Never went near the sea. Never went near water at all. Hated the stuff.

And then, when he'd had another drink or so, he told me why.

Before he came to Cornwall, Howells used to work in a water-works on the outskirts of London. He was on the maintenance staff, night shift. Once you got used to the hours, he said, it wasn't so bad. He used to work with a mate, a younger man, called Chris, proper Cockney type with a sharp tongue and a lively wit. They'd go round inspecting the various water plants, but most of the night they'd be sitting in the main engine room where the larger turbines and the purifying machines were pounding away.

Howells never liked the engine room from the beginning. It was an enormous building, painted throughout a brilliant white and flooded with highly powerful electric lighting. There was something merciless about that lighting, he said. It seemed to spotlight and reveal everything, so that there was no shelter at all. Just the light and the bare white walls and the steel floors – and the machines.

It was the machines upon which Howells' attention became focussed. Although, officially, he was in charge of the machines, he began to feel more and more the emptiness, indeed the impotence, of his position. The great revolving wheels, the plunging shining pistons, the whirring camshafts – there was something inevitable about their movement. In all the five years he was on night duty the machines never once stopped their relentless journey. Not until – (and there he pulled himself up, and shivered).

Sometimes he tried to explain these feelings to Chris, but he soon discovered that Chris had quite a different outlook on the machines. He used to joke about them, treat them in fact rather like a master might have treated very inferior servants in the Victorian days. His little pets, he would call the big twin-turbines, and he'd give names to some of the other enormous creations of steel. But there was something terribly contemptuous about Chris's attitude. He made it so evident that to him machines were just tools and slaves, just instruments abjectly designed to serve man's purposes.

Howells couldn't feel like that. As he sat there, night after night, lulled by the rhythmic hissing and pounding, he would often fall into a half-doze, and it was only too easy in that state to get the machines into quite a different focus. To Howells, from quite an early time, the machines were very real things, very alive things – very human things.

A silly idea perhaps? Yes, that was what Chris said, when he tried to express himself to the younger man. And when he persisted, Chris pointed derisively to nuts and bolts, to wire screws, green number plates, steel bars. Could they *talk*? he would jeer. And then he'd tell Howells to stop believing in fairies, and so on.

But perhaps the machines could talk? That was the sort of idea that drifted into Howells' mind, in those nightly reveries. And, indeed, try as he would to rationalise, he couldn't help thinking that sometimes the hissing and the thumping formed into queer, unrhythmical patterns – into voices.

He began to wonder if his mind was going, and he was afraid to tell Chris. But somehow, almost as if for devilment, the younger man seemed to go out of his way to deride Howells' vague theories – and to ridicule the machines themselves. What were they but a lot of old junk, he scoffed. Without a man to shape and fashion them, they'd be useless. And so on.

Somehow, Howells didn't feel easy about Chris going on like this. Perhaps some sixth sense was at work on him. And then, one night – well, he could have sworn that the crashing noise of the turbines and pistons spelt out a message. Da-di-da-di-di-di-da-di-da – quite what it meant, Howells couldn't be sure. But he could have sworn – and indeed he would still swear – that the hissing undertones spat out the name 'Chris'. And there was such an underlying, concentrated venom about the sound that he found himself impelled, against his conventional judgment, to warn Chris.

Against what, jeered Chris. Against these old bits of iron? And to show what a lot of nonsense old Howells was talking he began, perversely, to taunt the machines. He began, and this frightened Howells more than anything, to treat the machines with even less respect than before – even to the extent of becoming careless in his treatment of them. There were certain regulations and safety precautions which Chris and Howells were supposed to observe – but now Chris seemed to become deliberately offhand, even reckless. And if Howells remonstrated with him, he just laughed out aloud, and the laughter rose up and echoed about the white building, for a moment drowning even the sound of the machines.

It was the laughter, Howells always believed, that brought about the – happening. Chris was laughing out, loud and impudently, on that last evening. Howells tried to stop him. Something, some instinct, told him that there was something strange and sinister in the air. He could remember it now, how the building was so white and pitiless, how the lights blazed more fiercely than ever, and how, or so it seemed, the noises of the machines took on a dull, unfamiliar rumble, a rumble that beat into a steady thunder.

It was so very like a storm building up, approaching, growing in magnitude, that in a way Howells was only half surprised when the final lightning struck. Only – it wasn't lightning. No, it was one of the hydraulic-propelled pistons, a massive steel battering ram. Howells was too dazed by the thundering noise to remember exactly what happened. It did seem to him that though Chris was leaning over the safety railings, he was quite clear of the piston – and yet a moment later there was a terrible thud, and an impression of a gigantic shadow flying across the whiteness as the crumpled body was hurtled across the room and through an enormous glazed glass window, into space and eternity.

Yes, said Howells to me that evening, putting down his glass with a sigh, Chris's body was catapulted right out of the engine room – into one of the water wells. It was a nasty business fishing him out, too. That was why he never liked to go near water any more, he could only think of the water that was the last resting place of Chris.

But I could tell it wasn't really water that had scared old Howells so much. I could tell that something had happened that night, or he thought it had happened, that had shaken his whole being. Something to do with machines that became alive, and had voices – and dealt ruthlessly with their puny makers. It would be a terrifying idea, if brooded upon. You could well understand that, for a man who had been through such an experience, not even the remotest hamlet in Cornwall could really provide escape. Who knew but that behind those deceptive hills, the machines were gathering and multiplying, massing their armies for the final conquest of that fragile mankind which thought itself master – but perhaps soon would be slave.

The odd thing is that about a year later a runaway car careered down the village hill and knocked old Howells over, killing him instantly. The car – it was driverless – ran on for another quarter of a mile before finally smashing into a stone wall. The brakes had slipped and it had rolled down a slope into the hill of its own volition. Its runaway journey was quite unpremeditated, quite, quite purposeless.

And yet ... who knows?

V

The Lover

Mrs Wilson acquired herself a lover accidentally, you might say. It was all Polly Miller's fault, really. Polly was one of a group of young women who had grown up together in the district – they had played together, gone to school together, and of course flirted together with most of the eligible boys. In the end, in the way of things, they had got themselves married and settled down into varying states of wedded bliss.

All, this is, except Polly Miller. While the others had accepted their place in the inevitable pattern of things, duly producing their proud contributions to the future of the human race, Polly Miller had remained unrepentantly single and enviably free. Since she was a buxom and pretty little thing she continued to lead a gay and indeed delightful life, with as many dates and suitors as she wanted – a state of affairs which her married friends could hardly avoid noting, sometimes, rather sourly.

Polly had taken to calling on Mrs Wilson sometimes for an early afternoon cup of tea and chat, and it was during these pleasant tête-à-têtes that her fondness for elaborating on her romantic adventures began to rile her very much married hostess. It wasn't that Mrs Wilson begrudged Polly her romances so much as that she resented her obvious freedom to indulge in them. Yes, it was really too bad, it wasn't fair, it just wasn't fair.

Feeling like this – aware always of her own inevitable routine, getting husband and children off to work and school and then preparing for their regular return – it was hardly surprising that sometimes Mrs Wilson felt quite irritable as

Polly rambled on. Until finally one afternoon, provoked out of her normal placidity, she uttered the fatal words.

'As a matter of fact … I have a lover myself.'

At first the words evidently didn't register and Polly's pretty, rather pert little mouth went on opening and shutting – then all at once it stayed open, wide.

'You – what?'

'Like I said,' went on Mrs Wilson doggedly. 'I have a lover.'

Once committed she saw no alternative, in the face of the flattering look of astonishment that had now completely silenced the loquacious Polly, to producing further evidence.

'He's terribly sweet – and very goodlooking, of course.'

'But how did it happen? I mean – why?'

Mrs Wilson opened her mouth, then paused a moment. Why would a married woman, quite content and happy, take a lover? Guiltily she consigned her husband Bill to the very back of her mind, leaving it more free to contemplate the more tedious aspects of married life. It was the drudgery, that was it – being tied to the home by endless housework – and the children with their incessant demands – why you felt trapped, really trapped, no life of your own … Yes, she found it was better when she worked herself up over these points. Soon you got into a mood where the prospect of having a lover really began to appeal.

'What's he like?' asked Polly eagerly. 'I mean, what does he *look* like?'

'Well … ' Hastily Mrs Wilson contemplated the sort of man she might envisage as a lover. 'He's tall, fair-haired – curly fair hair, very blue eyes – good looking in a, well, romantic sort of way. Definitely – ' she warmed to her subject. ' – definitely the sort of man you'd look at more than once.'

'Mmmmh,' said Polly, a little doubtfully. 'Well, I presume you must have done.'

Becoming conscious of Polly's gaze of unwilling but undoubted admiration Mrs Wilson could not resist a warm glow of satisfaction. Obviously here was a side of life quite beyond a single woman's capacity. After all, to be married *and* to have a lover – that was something out of the common run.

'But how on earth did you meet? I mean, you and Bill always seem so close. I hardly ever see you apart.'

'Er, yes, well you see … ' Mrs Wilson struggled to pull her thoughts together, 'It was here – while Bill was at work and the children at school.'

'*Here?*'

'Yes.' Mrs Wilson launched her imagination into the glorious unknown. 'He called one day, by mistake – he was trying to find someone else's house, you see, and he knocked here to inquire, and then – well, somehow … '

As her story rambled on, a part of Mrs Wilson, curiously detached from her everyday self, saw the whole inviting scene – the door opening to reveal the tall, exciting presence of this unknown man destined, at a moment's notice, to become so important in her life. A tall man, indeed, his stranger's personality seeming everywhere – a personality that at once stirred something deep down inside of her. He had kind eyes, kind and gentle eyes that looked at her softly, as if understanding exactly how she felt. When he smiled at her and bowed slightly she felt – like a queen. Yes, just like a queen!

'Er, what?' said Mrs Wilson, suddenly aware of Polly addressing her.

'I said – aren't you frightened of being found out? Especially if you meet here – why, anyone might notice.'

'Oh, well, you see … ' Mrs Wilson's awakened mind was away again. After that first unforgettable occasion, when their eyes had been almost afraid to meet, their hands longing to touch – oh, it had been impossible not to see him again, the pain would have been intolerable. But it would indeed have been too dangerous and complicated for him to come to the house. Tongues might have wagged …

So they arranged to meet in the rambling park on the out-skirts of the town – by the bridge over the duck pond, yes, that was it. She could see him now, standing there and watching her gravely – how distinguished he looked, and yet somehow already rather familiar. A man of sophistication and poise, wise and understanding, a man of the world – the perfect lover. How graciously he came forward to greet her, taking her hand in his and pressing it gallantly to his warm lips ...

And then they turned and began walking arm in arm around the park, talking to each other in the low intimate tones of people destined to meet in such circumstances. On and on they walked, each circuit of the park representing another confidence, another shared memory, another web in the romantic net drawing them together. Oh, but wasn't this all part of the exhilaration of secret love? – certainly it gave a new zip to life, the world seemed brighter and more colourful, you could see that.

'Well, I never did!' exclaimed Polly, and Mrs Wilson could not help noticing the twinge of envy in her friend's voice.

'Sit down, Polly,' she said pleasantly. 'Have another cup of tea.'

Yes, indeed, for once in a way it was to be Polly Miller who listened with bated breath and respectful envy while she, stuffy old married Mrs Wilson, held the floor.

It was a pleasant experience and Mrs Wilson was understandably loath to give it up lightly. In fact she had little difficulty in keeping an open-mouthed Polly literally glued to her seat for the next half hour while she indulged, with growing expertise, in an imaginative account of her tumultuous secret love affair ... ranging from fairly innocent assignments in the corporation park to possibly less innocent gatherings in the secluded flat now occupied by her lover (married, of course, but misunderstood by and separated from his wife).

Every now and then Polly's eyes widened and her mouth went rounder and emitted an 'Oh!' or an 'Ah!' and sometimes an 'Ooooh!' – whereupon Mrs Wilson felt encouraged to new heights of invention.

'Of course, between you and me he's always on about running away together – he's very romantic, you see, oh, very romantic indeed.' She gave a modest laugh. 'You know, like in the olden days – a ladder at the window, that sort of thing.'

And for a moment, perhaps a magic moment, she even saw that really rather improbable scene – by silvery moonlight, of course, herself being borne away by the fair-haired stranger, away into the night, into some rather unimaginable world. Oh, it really was rather exciting.

'Well, I suppose I must be going.'

Rather unwillingly it seemed, Polly Miller got to her feet. She stood looking down, a little incredulous still, at safely settled Mrs Wilson. She shook her head in annoyance, as if still unwilling to acknowledge her own temporary eclipse.

'I would never have believed it – you of all people.'

Mrs Wilson allowed herself the pleasure of an ambiguous shrug of the shoulders.

'Who knows?' If she had had a long cigarette holder she would have taken a puff and blown out intriguing smoke rings: as it was she contented herself with a quizzical raising of the eyebrows. 'Who knows indeed?'

When Polly had finally gone Mrs Wilson felt a little guilty about the deception. Of course it served Polly right to be given a dose of her own bragging. All the same, she was bound to take the first opportunity to pass on such a juicy bit of gossip … ah, well, fortunately everyone knew Polly was a gossip, and no one was going to belive such a far-fetched fantasy about a happily married woman.

Mrs Wilson was still lost in her thoughts when she was startled by an unexpected ring at the front door bell. Still thinking about the afternoon's rather amusing interlude she padded down the corridor and opened the door.

'Yes?'

The man standing outside was tall and fair-haired, rather good-looking, even distinguished – but, of course, a complete stranger. And yet – Mrs Wilson stared in sudden alarm. Was he really a stranger?

'Excuse me, I'm sorry to trouble you, but I'm trying to find friends of mine, and I'm not quite sure of the right number. Perhaps you can kindly help me?'

For a moment, as the stranger looked quizzically across her familiar doorway, Mrs Wilson hovered, incredulously, between fantasy and reality. Afterwards she could never be quite sure, everything was so confused – but there did seem to have been a moment when perhaps there was an invitation in the stranger's eyes, some unspoken question – or was it all a myth?

Then, sanity returning, she provided the requisite information. 'Oh, yes, you want Number 41, that's left turn and about a hundred yards up on the opposite side.' ... and the stranger departed, with profuse thanks.

But somehow it wasn't until early that evening – when the front door burst open in the familiar way and her husband Bill was home, full of breezy talk about the day's events, and it suddenly seemed perfectly natural to tell him the whole amusing story of the spoofing of Polly Miller – that Mrs Wilson really felt at ease again. And even then, she couldn't help noticing, she left out the last little bit about the unexpected caller. It wasn't – she reflected, sitting contentedly enough with Bill's arm around her as they watched the television that evening – that she was anything less than a very happily married woman, with a dear and devoted husband. No, it was just that – well, perhaps it didn't do any harm, sometimes to remind yourself of what could happen – just so that you could realise how glad you were that it never would.

VI

Carnal Knowledge

When I was about seventeen we moved into a house on Wimbledon Common. In the house next door lived a Methodist preacher, his wife and their daughter. The preacher was a tight-lipped, hunched up little man who walked about with his head held downward and his hands clasped, unctuously, behind his back. His wife seemed little, too, or perhaps she had grown little in his company; she had wispy brown hair and delicate features, carrying with her the ghostly suggestion of one-time beauty, now buried beneath old-fashioned clothes, her secretive air. When the two of them walked along the street they seemed to shrivel up together, confronting the world with the tight-packed, impenetrable wall of their prejudiced outlook. They preached love of God, but I perceived even then that they represented the mean, the narrow and the intolerant.

The daughter was perhaps fifteen, too young yet to be finally contaminated. She was already taller than her parents, a loose-limbed buxom girl who seemed to be bursting out of her schoolgirl clothes. Indeed I had already overheard my mother make the comment that it was time Barbara, that was the girl's name, was treated as a girl and not a baby. I suppose what she meant was, dressed according to her age, and prepared in other ways for approaching womanhood. But, then, one felt that it would be the primary object of the parents to hide her from the world's evils as long as possible, to shield her eyes just as they attempted to shield her body – though no doubt with an equal lack of success.

Beyond a nodding acquaintance any contact between myself

and the girl next door was not encouraged. And so, officially, there was none. But there remained the inevitable, secret, overt relationship. We would pass each other in the street; one of us, looking out of a window, would catch the eye of the other strolling in the garden; or a voice would be heard, an image recalled. I do not suppose there was any special attraction. But there was curiosity, and no doubt the implied censorship of her parents gave everything an air of illicit excitement. We never spoke directly about the matter, but each time we passed, each time our glances met, we were instinctively aware of all that remained unsaid, and perhaps more.

One day, crossing the common, I met Barbara taking her dog for a walk, and for a few minutes stood talking rather shyly. From nowhere, it seemed, her father appeared, sour-faced and aggressive, almost tugging her away from the danger of my presence. I was left feeling upset, rather stupid; and angry, too. I could not help feeling how awful for her, how humiliating; and in my anger I was stirred to action, and I determined to see her again if only to spite her father.

As I had guessed, a similar spirit of rebellion had been provoked in Barbara. It was not long before an accidental meeting gave us the chance to speak again. Then it was we made the first of a number of clandestine arrangements for meeting. On that occasion, I think, we went on different buses to Kingston and had an evening by the river, watching the punts and canoes gliding past, and the occasional paddle steamer laden with singing trippers.

It was strange, but we did not talk a great deal, nor to any extent pursue inquiries about one another. It was as if to be together, in defiance of irrational orders to the contrary, was enough in itself. We did not discuss either her parents or mine. It was rather as if we wished to be solitary beings, just encountered, whose purpose was to bring some sort of liberation, a freedom.

At the same time, inevitably, we became physically aware of one another. Sometimes while walking, I took her arm, or she held my hand; or perhaps crossing a gate, her thick dark hair brushed against my face softly. The sensation was a momentary one; but pleasant, and curiously enriching. More than that I do not think it had any great meaning for me. But looking back I can see that the thing ran deeper for Barbara, and that this physical awakening held a special importance for her, as a symbol of her possible freedom from the shackles of her nonconformist background.

That was not how I thought then, of course, I was far too young and naive. All the same I did notice that sometimes she eyed me in a strangely contemplative way, almost as our beautiful, remote black cat would sit and stare ... a wise and confident sort of contemplation. I remember I had the sense of some subterranean purpose and intention behind her gaze.

One afternoon, meeting in the street, Barbara touched my arm gently.

'You can come and see me this evening, if you like. My father is preaching over at Hounslow, and mother is going too. I shall be all alone. Will you come?'

I can recall the exact words even now, for they were said with such tremendous meaning. It was, in effect, a command more than a request. I knew that come what may, I had to go. I knew, I suppose, that she needed me.

All the same, when I tapped at the front door, I could feel my body cold and almost trembling. I suppose I was as nervous as the girl who now opened the door and forced a casual smile.

'Come in ... '

Inside, the hall was dark, after the brightness outside. Only when my eyes became accustomed to the subdued light did I notice the change in Barbara. She no longer had on her schoolgirl clothes, but wore a dressing gown, tied tight around the waist with a cord. Her hair, which was usually wound round in pigtails, was loose and flowing, and falling right down her back. She seemed suddenly almost another person, and I was a little afraid of what to do next.

But Barbara seemed cool and sure of herself. First she showed me round the house, which was not very interesting. Then she took me into the one nice room, a sitting-room with french windows opening out on to the garden.

'Shall we sit down?'

I looked around.

'Here,' she went on. 'On the couch.'

It was a big old-fashioned couch into which we seemed to sink, as in to a sea.

I was conscious not only of Barbara close beside me, but that as she sat down the neck of her dressing gown had opened, to reveal the white skin beneath.

She must have seen my glance, for she smiled, and a faint touch of colour showed in her cheeks. Then she spoke my name softly, in a way I had never heard before, and she asked:

'Have you ever kissed a girl?'

I suppose I had, at parties and so on. But I knew that was not what she meant.

'Have you?'

I shook my head. She looked at me steadily. Her face was soft and strongly formed, and her eyes seemed crystal clear. I saw for the first time the intimations of womanly beauty. I wanted to say something, but the words would not come. I felt myself drawn irresistibly towards those steady eyes, those waiting lips.

Our kiss was a clumsy, experimental one. The next one was better. We sat back, a little out of breath, flushed, considerably excited.

'Barbara … ' I said, and stopped. What else was there to say?

She did not answer. But she spoke my name again, and somehow gave it an endearing sound.

It was then that she stretched forward her plump, determined hands, and took hold of mine – and drew them towards that fold in her dressing gown.

'Will you touch – my breasts?'

Even as she asked the question she was prompting my hands under her dressing gown. I felt, with a shock, the warmth, the softness, the desirability of her bare young flesh. I followed the curves, the suppleness. In a moment, almost unconsciously, I was fondling the young, delicate breasts, hanging forward like the proverbial pears.

It was then that some of her own confidence entered into

me, and perhaps instinctively I realized what to do. Slowly her dressing gown seemed to slip forward and off the round white shoulders, until it had fallen down and down, down to the swell of her thighs. I behold the beauty revealed with wondering eyes, touching her gently, tracing with marvelling fingers, the geography unfolded before my youthful eyes. All this time Barbara did not speak, but smiled strangely: I knew she was pleased.

Finally she was completely naked, and lay relaxed along the couch, while with great gentleness I stroked her body from end to end, seriously and carefully, and with sensual pleasure.

'Ah,' she said. 'Ah ... that is beautiful, beautiful. I feel ... '

She did not say what she felt, but in a way I knew. She felt released and liberated, she felt free. She had taken some sort of action that had brought to her a change, there would be no going back, there could be no obliteration. At her bequest I had awakened the sleeping powers, and she was, even in that moment, no longer the schoolgirl.

Perhaps ... but it was at this point that the front door key turned, the door opened, and within a few seconds our intimate, secret scene was exposed to the shocked and horrified gaze of her parents.

It was an unpleasant moment. The little man shouted and raved. His wife wept, Barbara said nothing. In the end I went, rather miserable. In my ears rang the preacher's threats:

'I'll have you up for this! I'll go to the police! I'll take you to court. It's an offence, you know. Carnal knowledge ... '

Nothing actually happened. Shortly afterwards, Barbara left home and took a job somewhere. I never saw her again. But I am glad she found her freedom. It gives me a warm sort of glow each time I remember, to know that in some way I was instrumental in her finding herself. My only regret, on looking back, is that I did not in fact, in the strict sense of the word, enjoy to the full that carnal knowledge of which her father spoke. It would have been an illuminating experience.

VII

River of Light

The river of light flows under Llantyllan bridge, hissing and spraying and tumbling over gleaming stones. Somewhere it must have been a single round raindrop and somewhere it will sink into the infinity of an ocean, but there, under Llantyllan bridge, where the road winds up from the village towards the mountain farms, it is green and white and golden – a river of light. It bubbles with wet laughter and sings with the morning breeze, and somehow it is alive and afire, as if kissed by the sun and the moon and a thousand winking stars. Look deep into its shining waters and you will see, mirrored, all your lifetimes and all your loves.

It has always been so, and that is how it was for Curigwen, who used to walk across the mountainside every morning, sitting herself on the wide stone parapet and watching the waters live and die. Curigwen, who was young and warm and afire, like the river, with her Welsh darkness and her Welsh loveliness, and with her heart in the smile of her face. Curigwen, who was fresh as the mountain air and as brown as the bracken-berries, her hair like sunshine and her eyes wet and shining, like rock around Llantyllan.

Curigwen was born high up on the mountainside, in a squat ugly, quarryman's cottage, half under the shadow of the quarry-head and a long way from the sound of water. But when she was still small her mother strapped her across her shoulder, in an old brown shawl, and carried her on the long journey across the fields into Llantyllan for shopping. One day, when the burden seemed extra heavy, she came on to a bridge, breathing heavily from weariness, and sank down for a rest, laying the child along the top of the warm parapet. Then, perhaps, Curigwen first knew the sound of water, and that it lived and died as it flowed under Llantyllan bridge. Then, though a child's sleepy eyes might see no more of the world than the blue-flecked whiteness of a mother's sagging breasts, yet a child's old ears might hear the hiss of water on stone and recognise the music of a thousand years. So it was for Curigwen then – then, and later, when she was old enough to come across the mountainside on her own, with her pigtails and rounded cheeks and her thin brown legs sticking out like tree branches ... When she was old enough and tall enough to stand tiptoe and peep over the edge of the parapet, seeing the new rippling, singing, winking world.

Curigwen knew it was the river of light the first time she went alone down to Llantyllan bridge. A morning in April, not long after the rains, the old stones of the bridge still wet and glistening. She came with her old shopping bag over her arm and a long shopping list in her mind, and then she climbed high on to the parapet, and leant over, and all was forgotten. There it was, the river of light, bubbling and laughing with joy – a great sheet of gold carved from the newly budded sun, high and far away. There was fire in the water, and smoke in the spray, and a life and a light in the long spiralling cascade, dancing with wild lover's abandonment on its journey towards the great embrace of the waiting sea.

Curigwen stood on Llantyllan bridge that day and opened her eyes wide – and because she was young and beautiful and innocent so, too, she opened wide her body and her mind and her soul, her whole warm life – and she felt the river of light come streaming into her, and all over her like rain from the Heavens. There was a hissing and spraying, a murmuring and singing, and she was washed clean and good and pure and wet with morning happiness.

She looked deep, deep down into the waters, and saw, smiling, age-old pools of life – she looked deeper and deeper, and saw waterfalls of sunshine and laughter, mountains of light and joy. She laughed with the laughing river, tossed it a kiss, and then went her way down into the village. She sang at the top of her voice and all the shopkeepers looked at her in amazement and wonder. They paid her the compliments of the morning and gave her their special luxuries, for she had suddenly become alive and the most beautiful girl in Llantyllan.

After that Curigwen used to come walking over to Llantyllan bridge every morning, rain or fine. First, though, she would see to sending her father to the quarry, and tidying up the cottage and starting the broth boiling for lunch, for by now her mother's face was old and tired and she seldom rose from her wicker bed-chair in a corner of the living room. Then, at last, Curigwen would come out and climb over a rusty gate and set off across the soft brown peat carpet of the mountainside, turning away from the grey quarry-head. She walked with a slow careless swing of her body, her hair loose in the morning breezes and her face brown and thrown upwards to the sun. She walked over the fields and the bracken and the granite, down to the river of light – to sit with the sun kissing her back and her legs dangling deep over the water – to dream and to wish and to be drowned again with new life.

When she was still a schoolgirl Curigwen used to sit on Llantyllan bridge for hours, blinking lazily at the flowing river. She looked at the waters and saw the hundred colours of a rainbow, the thousand shades of a sky, the million winks a star – saw the sun and the moon, the green and the blue of the sea, and even the gold of some faraway sands. She let the river of light come tumbling down from the mists of the mountains, let it flow into her and through her and as it did so she could feel within her the beginning and end of everything.

Sometimes she would just lie dreaming, but sometimes she would sit up and hold her arms out to the river, making her prayers and her wishes. She wished often that the warmth and the love of the river of light be given to her mother, tired in a cottage bed, and that the kindness and sweetness of the river be given to her father, angry and bitter at his quarry pit. Sometimes it seemed as if the wish was drowned in the river and forgotten, but other times she went home and kissed her mother and smiled at her father, and there was something of the old happiness about the three of them ... And sometimes Curigwen wished to herself, wished that she might do well at her lessons and please the local mistress, who was tall and sharp-nosed and a spinster, and who always frowned at her. She wished that the music teacher would choose her for the choir singing – or she wished she could be invited to Miss Pritchard's tea party. Now and then she wished long and earnestly that she might always be young and that she might become beautiful – but on those occasions the hiss and the spray vanished like smoke, the waters were suddenly calm and smooth like the most perfect mirror, and, seeing herself, Curigwen knew in her heart that the last wish was hers forever.

Curigwen grew fifteen and sixteen, and then seventeen and eighteen, and at last nineteen, and with her growing the beauty blossomed and spread out like a flower. Curigwen at nineteen, with her hair done up and glinting, with the summer colour upon her cheeks – there was the sight of Llantyllan, a Welsh beauty again, as the old men of the village said when she went past. So it was perhaps natural that now, when she sat beside the river of light, she dreamed different dreams, had wishes that were not quite the same as those of the distant schoolgirl. For Curigwen now had a full round heart and a woman's early passion, and there was a new rosy flush to her face as she sat dreaming on Llantyllan bridge. And when she was like that the river of light seemed to whirl and dance and sparkled more than ever before. The spray seemed to fly higher than ever before, forming great white misty shapes. Sometimes, or so Curigwen thought, with a blush and a turn of her head, the shapes took form, merged into new, yet familiar outlines. Sometimes the cascading river of light smiled at her knowingly, and filled the air with strange visions ... Old knights in armour, rough shepherds from the mountains, dark-skinned troubadours, tall young princes ... Those were the times when Curigwen looked into the heart of the river of light and whispered softly and shyly that someday, not too far away, there might come to her a man and a lover.

But it had to be a king among men for a woman like Curigwen and there were many shy and abashed men of

Llantyllan village, as the sun came and went and the moons rode high on summer skies, before at last came the only one. He came unexpectedly, as perhaps only Curigwen could have thought for him to come. One morning she lay dreaming into the river, and then, there he was … brown in the face and hard looking from the land, with his old coat over his shoulder and a stout stick under his arm … standing down beside the flowing river and looking up into Curigwen's wide open eyes. It didn't matter what his name was (though it was in fact Ioanto, from old Wales) and it didn't matter where he came from, or why. It only mattered that he was there and that Curigwen looked into his eyes and knew. While the hissing and the spraying sank down and the river of light seemed to melt away, leaving only Curigwen and Ioanto, on Llantyllan bridge. Then, indeed, with Llantyllan asleep and still at peace, was life complete. Then was the whole troubled world a smiling Welsh village. The mountains afire with life and love, the river singing like the birds. The sun high in the heavens and the wind free among the trees, the smoke of the houses warm and friendly, like the smiles of the villagers – the tempo of living the beat of two hearts.

Now it was Curigwen swinging across the mountainside, and Ioanto waiting at the top of the road, and a seat for two on the warm bridge. Sometimes in the sun-showered mornings, and sometimes in the dozing afternoons, but always in the evening, with one light dying and another being born. With the stars alive a thousand times in the night sky, with the waters drifting silently out of the valley woods and across the stones, and under Llantyllan bridge. Then was the river of light the river of love, then was a lifetime fulfilled. Those days, I tell you, Llantyllan stood still, the folk walked about with rich smiles, and by the day and by the night few ever went near the bridge at the top of the village. A sun all the day and a moon all the night, the river flowing swifter and sweeter than ever, and stones gleaming the colours of all life. Time when Curigwen lay with Ioanto and they were bathed anew by the river of light. Time when a thousand years' loves sprang out of the old, old stones and out of the ageless waters. Time when the river of light flowed under Llantyllan bridge like a fire and burnt a path to eternity.

But follow the river back to the mountains and see it disappear into a stone, follow the river down to the waves and see it swallowed by an ocean, and remember the ticking of time on a grandfather clock. Count the ebb and flow of the years, like the tides, and listen afar for the sad faint murmur of men's thunderguns. See the lights dimmed in Llantyllan, one after another, the seas filled with strange ships and the air broken with battleblast, the faces of the villagers no longer smiling, but sad and weary. As Curigwen sees this, and weeps – as Ioanto sees this, and feels the forthcoming pain deep in his heart. Clouds in the air, and in the life; rain in the sky, and in lovers' eyes; fields suddenly empty and barren, like hearts for the future. Only one beginning and only one ending and only one pathway. Till the time, now as before, when a man with brown skin and rough hair springs out of the stone bridge of Llantyllan, steel heart and steel face. Not looking back and not looking sideways, but striding away to a new war and a new world.

Then was the time when time was timeless, then was the time when the shadows hovered over Llantyllan bridge, then was the time when Curigwen came alone and went alone and the river of light flowed quiet and afraid to smile. The nights black and the days empty and the heart as heavy as the mountains. Only the occasional faint glimmer of memory, mirrored in water – only the sudden sweetness and sadness of a picture, a word, a thought, from a thousand miles across the world – only, real and yet unreal, the faint movement of a new life, sweet and warm in the womb ... Oh, voiceless old stones that can speak and yet will not speak! Oh, heedless old waters that are living and yet dying, coming and yet departing! Oh, the memory of love in a wet stone, in a spray of water, in a kiss of the sun! Someday a life and someday my lover, wished the old Curigwen, weeping and alone by the river.

But the river of light flowed faster and darker, grew dull and grey and lost to the sun ... and one day it reared up, in the mountainholds, and came rushing down to Llantyllan swollen and overladen, as if with tears. One day there was fear in its eyes and thunder in its ears and pain twisting its heart. One day the river of light flowed under Llantyllan bridge, darker, and there were long warm streaks of redness painted on its quivering waters. That day it flowed down to the sea like the blood from a man's life and the tears from a woman's heart.

Such a day there never has been and never will be, since that day when the sun hid behind the clouds, the great rains washed over the mountains, and the river of light swept in mourning colours down to the sea. The river of light was the river of death, its warmth was the cold of ice and its heart was the echo of stones. The river washed under Llantyllan bridge like a great sea of sorrow, on down to the dry-eyed oceans, and its laughter was tears and its singing was weeping.

When the sun had set and the night had fallen, and when a new day dawned with the brightness of new life, there was only an empty Llantyllan bridge, and a sad old river. The river of light flowed under Llantyllan bridge like before and like after, but in a moment of time the river had risen up and embraced its Curigwen and borne her away, and now forever she was asleep in the vast oceans, drowned for the shroud of her lover. And he cold and empty in a far land.

Stand on Llantyllan bridge, now, and look into the river and you may see only the brightness of dancing water. But look deep and deeper, and it may be you will see there are tears in the water and blood-spots on the stones. Look deeper still and you will, some time, see all the colours of the rainbow – and far away in the river of light, mirrored, all your lifetimes and all your loves.

VIII

The Man I Killed

Foster remained very still as he studied the man he was going
to kill. Everything about the man was excessively, indeed
irritatingly familiar – the inevitable brown suede coat, the
cock-sparrow felt hat with a feather stuck jauntily in the brim,
the smart yet somehow slightly vulgar check-pattern trousers,
the patent-leather shoes ... The man was a cheap show-off;
there was nothing else to be said.

However, this wasn't exactly why he was going to kill him.
Foster pursed his lips and looked thoughtfully along the line of
the gun barrel. The reasons for his impending action were
really too diverse to sum up in a sentence or two. If they had to
be condensed into a phrase then he supposed it might be called
a case of retribution.

He smiled quietly at the rather ironical thought, but did not
take his eyes off the image of his victim. The man sat
apparently calm and relaxed, looking not at all like someone
with only a short time left to live. He was a man in his early
forties, with superficial good looks which hid, momentarily, an
unmistakable shallowness – it was the face of someone who
lived too much on his wits, too little by his heart.

'You cocky bastard!' thought Foster with sudden venom,
and for a moment he was tempted to get it over with there and
then, but prudence held his hand. He knew that the woman
who came in to do the cleaning was still moving around
downstairs; it was essential to wait until she had gone.

He thought about the slow, deliberate planning that had led
up to this situation – obtaining the fire-arms certificate,
acquiring the ammunition and all the other apparatus, and

then keeping everything safely hidden from prying eyes. At first it had been worrying, even frightening – but latterly the whole affair had begun to fascinate him.

After all, he thought, curiously, his eyes turning constantly from the gun to his victim, the thing had a certain macabre touch to it that would hardly fail to appeal. Some killings were claimed to be justified, other were excused as self-defence, a few were perhaps genuine accidents – in most cases the killers were inevitably caught and punished. This was one case which was going to be foolproof; the killer would never be caught.

He contemplated the shiny barrel of the gun, steadfastly in line with the man's head. For a moment, as he imagined the actual physical result of the explosion, his hand wavered and a shiver ran through his body. But then, he told himself this was not the moment to lose heart.

Instead, to revive his killer's instinct, he began to think about all the things which the man had done – bad things, cruel things, quite inexcusable things. He remembered becoming aware of him in the Army in the war, a coward at heart without the guts to be even a conscientious objector – and the time he had turned and run abjectly when he could have helped a dying comrade. And then afterwards, because of his superficial good looks, how he had talked his way into a succession of high-pressure selling jobs – well, he supposed he had not been a bad salesman, of a sort. It was an attribute that proved very effective in other ways, too: the number of women the man had casually seduced and then left stranded could be counted on the fingers of several hands.

And then there had been Eve. That had been unforgivable – for that alone the swine deserved to die. Eve had been the only daughter of a nice old-world couple who, when they died, had left her quite a sum of money. The man had known about this and made a dead-set at the girl – only this time, for practical reasons, he decided it was a suitable occasion for marriage.

They were married with a great amount of show, arranged for by the man but paid for by Eve, and then they moved into Eve's parents' former home. There the man had lived a comfortable life for years, waited on hand and foot by a doting wife who seemed utterly blind to his obvious faults – even when, inevitably for such a man, he began to conduct discreet affairs with other women.

The man stirred, and Foster moved too. He wondered if it were possible that even a man so vulgar and self-centred might not have some psychic awareness of his impending fate. He studied the still handsome but visibly ravaged face for some signs, noticing at the moment of close inspection those further signs of weakness – the baby lips, the close set of the eyebrows, the unexpected hardness of the blank grey eyes. No, this was hardly the countenance of a man repentant and ready to meet his Maker.

And yet – and yet – Foster hesitated, a strange warm pain prickling at his eyeballs as he remembered. There had been times when even such a man, yes, even such a man ... he remembered, inconsequentially, a carefree ramble over the downs, wind blowing in the hair, a gaiety of laughter ... another occasion, years ago, bathing in the sea in Cornwall, just like a child, with all those worldly cares forgotten ... At such times, surely even such a man had been a curiously human being, worthy of some love?

And then another picture came to Foster's mind – of the man with his small son, then only a mite of about two years old, a surprisingly pretty little boy who had obviously adored his father – and, to give him his due, his father had obviously felt the same. Foster had a vivid memory once of the two of them playing in the park; the little boy waddling across the green turf, arms outstretched, and being picked up by his father and whirled round and round and round ...

Wasn't there perhaps some excuse after all?

Foster shook his head slowly, half to himself, half at the man's image. Excuses were a short-term currency: they were never good value for a long-term loan. Besides, the man's wife and child had long since left him, driven away by his own selfish behaviour – for a time they had disappeared, but recently word had come that they had started a new life far away, in another country. Foster knew only too well that the man, once he had recovered some kind of Dutch courage, was quite capable of following them, intruding into their new life, perhaps ruining their chances of making a fresh start.

Suddenly Foster gave a start, hearing the bump of the front door as the woman closed it behind her and walked away down the garden path, leaving the house enveloped in a deathly silence. Well, then, there it was …

He swallowed hard and took a last look at the man he was going to erase from the face of the earth. Funny, but in this moment of extremity, his dominant feeling was simply one of pity. After all, everyone was a human being, everyone had desires and hopes, the same yearning for the intangible and marvellous magic of life. Everyone reached out, few grasped the precious fruit. This man had been like that, too, poor devil. It wasn't altogether his fault that he had turned out to be such a rotter. It wasn't altogether his fault that he was weak and vain, cowardly and cruel … And now look at him, left all alone and unloved in the world. Poor lonely devil …

'To hell with you, you miserable bag of self-pity?' shouted Foster in a last paroxysm of blind railing – against fate, against time, against truth.

Then with a decisive gesture he pressed the button of the long cord leading back to the gun fixed firmly on the tripod in front of the mirror facing him … and the gun fired, the bullet passing clean through the centre of Foster's forehead, as planned.

The verdict was suicide while of unsound mind.

IX

Such Sweet Sorrow

It was a short distance from the bus stop to the railway station. But to each of them it seemed an eternity: a distance it was impossible to travel – and yet which must be accomplished.

They walked in silence and apart. But even in their apartness, they were joined. The tall man walked with a slight stoop, as if hunched up in contemplation of some immense and unsolvable problem. Once he shook his head slightly then stared about him angrily, as if wondering what on earth he was doing here walking towards the distant echo of railway coaches, the occasional eerie whistle of a train.

The woman, short, slender, fair-skinned, pretty in a very English way, with her silvery-grey suede coat a pleasant contrast to the glory of her Titian hair, walked more deliberately and precisely. There was about her a curious resignation, almost a despair – yet she did not hesitate, nor look about her, and held her head high, as if she was determined to face the future at all costs.

They came into the station yard, dark except for a single light over the booking hall entrance, and in the distance the sombre yellow platform lights.

Both of them were thinking: surely this is all a dream; surely this can't be happening – to us.

They walked through their dream towards the poky aperture of the booking office, and while the woman stood irresolute the man fumbled awkwardly in his pocket and paid over the money for a single ticket.

As they moved towards the barrier they both looked at the big, rigid fingers of the station clock, quivering at ten minutes to the hour.

'The train's almost due,' the man said. Almost furtively he handed the ticket to the girl, then looked about him rather helplessly. It seemed as if by habit that at last he took his companion's elbow and ushered her on to the platform, where they joined one or two other uneasy spirits hovering among the ghostly yellowness.

'You'll be sitting down for quite a while,' the man said hesitantly. 'Perhaps we should walk up and down until the train comes?'

The woman nodded, and slowly fell into step, following the pattern of their journey up and down the long grey platform. It was, she thought, rather like an ebb and flow – rather as their life together had been. All their long life together, all that long and crowded, that vivid and memorable year together.

And now they were parting.

Far away a train whistle echoed and re-echoed, like a mournful dirge.

The sound played on their nerves, so that both of them started and stopped, and looked away from each other.

What on earth is happening to us? the man thought. He looked in bewilderment at the dimness, the bizarre lights, the unfamiliar setting. Why are we here? What are we doing? Is this really happening to me, to her – to us?

The woman asked no questions. Not any longer. She felt as if she was drained; she had nothing more to ask about. She was conscious only of a great weariness. They had battled for too long: now she had reached breaking point, she could fight no more, she could only go away.

'Do you remember – ?' he began; and then stopped. He bit his lip and tried to forget the bitter-sweet memory.

Yes, I remember everything, the woman thought. They had reached the end of the platform and in silent accord turned and began walking back again.

Yes, I remember the day we met. It was at a dance and I had never seen you before but you came over and asked me to dance, and I was frightened because the moment you held me in your arms I felt as if I had always belonged there. That was the wonderful thing about it, there was no beginning, no wondering, no hesitation – suddenly we were together, as if we had always been together.

Oh, yes, I remember it. And I remember so much else too. The day we were married, the honeymoon, the new house, the time we went on the river, the week-end by the sea, I remember, I remember … They were all like magic. And yet –

Sometimes, I suppose, people lose touch, the man thought. He dug his hands deeper into his macintosh pockets, a little angry, determined not to touch the woman, not to influence her in any way. If she felt she wanted to be free, then she must be so. Free of what? he pondered. Suddenly he wanted to cry, and he could not remember having cried since he was a child.

If only, the woman thought, if only he wouldn't try to possess me so much. If only he would understand part of me, a tiny part, must always remain separate, otherwise I cease to be me, to be myself. But he wouldn't, he couldn't. She knew that now. She knew he couldn't change – so she had to get away.

In the end it happened almost casually. They had one of their endless discussions, one of their eternal tussles, and in some way she was finally exasperated beyond endurance – quite suddenly she found herself announcing her decision. Perhaps there had been something in the way she spoke, in the tone of her voice: at any rate the man seemed to give way, to give up.

He just looked at her puzzledly and said: 'Yes, I suppose – if you really feel like that – it would be best. Yes, I do see that.'

If he had argued, if they had both gone on talking, even if they had wrangled about it, perhaps there might have been a better result. But the sore thing, the desperate thing was he had not disagreed or even tried to dissuade her. He had only shrugged and said: 'If you really feel you must go – ' And when the time came he had brought her to the station.

'I think I can hear the train,' the woman said dully.

The man turned and listened. Panic rushed through him as he realised the moment had come – the last terrible moment.

Mechanically he took the woman's elbow again. 'Mind you don't go too near the edge.'

She said nothing. She felt her voice had gone from her, and if she tried to speak she would burst into tears.

Mutely they stood back as the train drew in. It was an express to London and this was its last stop. In a few minutes it would vanish into darkness, like a rocket to another planet. Doors opened, voices were raised, passengers got out, others got in.

'Darling – ' The woman's voice was unsteady.

The man propelled her forward.

'Here's a carriage,' he said with a tonelessness of despair. 'You'll be comfortable here. You can sit with your back to the engine.'

He hurried her towards a doorway, then paused suddenly, remembering something, fumbling in his pockets.

'Oh, and by the way, here's some chocolate. You'll probably be glad of it on the journey.'

Somehow the woman found herself aboard the train, seated in an empty carriage, her back to the engine. In one hand was her ticket to London and freedom. In the other was a coloured bar of her favourite chocolate.

The man had disappeared down the train corridor. Now like a ghostly apparition, he loomed at the window, seeming to fill it entirely with his tall, familiar figure.

The woman blinked. Suddenly she stood up and went across and opened the window wide. Without their own volition their hands touched and pressed together: speaking what their voices could not say.

'Look after yourself,' the man said huskily at last.

He peered at her closely, seeing the fine-drawn features, the shadows round the eyes: the face he loved so dearly – the secret spirit of the person he had come to know.

Or had he? Was he perhaps only now, at this moment of parting, beginnng to know her? Now when for the first time in his life he knew the purity of love and gave her up sincerely to her own needs.

'Good-bye,' he said. He forced a faint smile, and stood back. Somewhere down the platform a green light showed, and the guard's whistle blew shrilly, ominously.

'Good-bye, my darling.'

As the train jerked into movement, the woman seemed to come to herself, out of some long, distant dream. It was as if all her life, all her love, had been compressed into an instant of time, a moment of truth. Everything unessential and unimportant seemed to fade away, burnt to cinders by this blinding flame of revelation.

Slowly the train began to move away.

Suddenly the woman was at the window, leaning out, looking beseechingly at the man who still walked beside the moving train.

'I love you.' Her eyes brimmed with tears. 'Darling, I always have done, I always will. I've tried to pretend I didn't but – ' She leaned farther out of the window as the train began to gather speed. 'Darling – I'll come back – the next train back – '

The man stopped walking. He stood and watched, and then he waved. His lips framed the answer: I'll be waiting.

He did not know if she heard, but he knew that she understood. Somehow he knew that they both understood this parting would be the beginning of something very wonderful.

X

The Perpetual Revolution

Burton first thought of the idea one autumn evening, driving home from the town to his country house, the big twin headlamps of his green sports car bathing the country lanes with a light more brilliant than any sun or moon. There was an immense sense of security sitting behind the wheel, wrapped in the remote secrecy of the car, the whole world pinpointed in the arcs of light. He was conscious of life throbbing in the wheel under his hands, of the warmth of his seclusion, the inevitability of his majestic journey across the hidden face of the night. It occurred to him, then, that the power was all his, that the switches and buttons that decided life might all be fixed on the gleaming dashboard so handily placed for a flick of his fingers.

Burton was a big, crisp sort of man, a director of his own chrome manufacturing concern. He had begun life as a salesman, selling anything and everything, and gradually he had pushed his way to the top. Now he did less selling, for the chrome was almost a necessity to engineers, aeroplane firms, makers of cars. He had become more interested in manufacturing than selling, in machines rather than words. He was fascinated with the efficiency of machines; and to a certain degree his own bluff, muscular self had acquired that same efficiency.

When he got home he practically ignored his wife, and spent most of the evening on the telephone. He rang up key men in the city, and some further afield. He was a man of varied talents and interests, he had friends in unexpected places, including the highest. He spoke quietly but persuasively, evoking one clear fact after another, carrying them along with him on the crest of the sudden wave of decisiveness. It did not occur to them, or him, to argue. They set into motion the first steps, the idea began to take practical shape. There were to be meetings, schedules, minutes, manifestoes, an advertising campaign. Large spaces, whole pages, were booked in the following day's newspapers. Burton had a friend, Glenser, in the advertising business, a genius at his work, loving and breathing it. He seized on Burton's idea for the world-shattering potential it was, and rammed into action.

In twenty-four hours the campaign was in full swing. Glenser had three printers working overtime to produce the enormous red and white posters that began to appear all over the country, at every street corner, along every main thoroughfare. In cities and towns teams of billboard men were organised and sent off into the streets, bearing their same red and white messages. By the evening halls had been booked, crowds had received their invitations, Burton and Glenser between them had even sent into action the first shock of troops of speakers. The next morning the papers were full of it; not just advertisements, but great column length stories, with banner headlines.

The League of Motorists was Burton's name for it, a well-chosen one. There was something friendly and attractive about the word league. It suggested comradeship, fair play, equal shares, the security of numbers. Motorists everywhere flocked to join, queueing up outside the emergency offices which were opened in every town and large village. Nothing much had been said yet about the organisation, there were not even any rules and regulations. Burton issued a statement that these were still being worked out – in the meantime every motorist who joined was given a bright new badge, a membership card, a leaflet announcing that an important statement of policy was to be expected within a short while. Motorists were urged to overhaul their cars, to ensure that they were in the best possible running order, to prepare themselves for any possible emergency.

The whole thing became intriguing. People were caught up by the same wave of part-exhilaration, part-fear that distinguished the reaction to the air bombings of the war, to other national events like Cup Finals, the Grand National, a Royal Marriage. Thousands rushed to buy cars so that they could qualify for membership. Some of the most fantastic old wrecks were unravelled from a heap of spare parts, dusted and polished, driven out into the forgotten daylight. Garages all over the country were besieged, stripped of their stock, new cars and old. In some places mechanical-minded youths began making their own cars from the gleanings of local scrap heaps.

Burton watched all this unperturbed. The important thing was the initial enthusiasm; the pruning out could come later – and indeed come it must, for the success of his plans. Now his own inbred sense of efficiency was a tremendous asset. It enabled him to carry it all forward, the tremendous organisation, the hundred and one administrative projects, in one steady movement. In five days it was all accomplished. The League's membership was total, not a motorist in the country without a card. The garages had been primed, secretly circulated, they awaited eagerly the dawn of an era of security such as they had never known. Burton had made several trips, to the Midlands, to London, to the West – in each area he had addressed a secret assembly of the main motor car manufacturers, and in each case his swift, factual persuasiveness had won them unhesitatingly to his side. Finally he had been busy on the cables, and the telephone, contacting the petrol combines, presenting their directors with his mounting list of unassailable facts. On the fifth day their signature of agreement came through – subject, of course, they stipulated, to Government approval.

Burton laughed when he read the note of caution. It was the ineffectual protest of all appeasers. He pushed it away into a reference file, and then picked up the telephone. He spoke to each of his area organisers. It was the word they had been waiting for. Then he replaced the telephone and went out to his garage. He opened the doors, climbed swiftly into the green sports car, backed it out into the drive and accelerated hard towards the ornamental gateways. Out of a top floor window his wife watched with sad eyes. She wondered if she would ever see him again.

Burton remembered once reading a book about a famous revolution, bearing the title: *Seven Days that Shook the World*. His own, conceived in the headlights of an evening's drive, took one day less. On the sixth day, the League of Motorists took over the country.

On the morning of that day every motorist received a leaflet headed in bold crimson type: 'Motorists of the World – Unite! '. Underneath were the few lines of instructions which were at once to become their creed, and relieve them from all the responsibilities that had hitherto constrained and burdened their variegated lives.

> Motorists, this is your great moment. The time has come when a machine-minded world must be organised by the men who understand the machines. For thousands of years corrupt politicians, priests and pedestrians have administered the world inefficiently and to their own ends. Today will witness the obliteration of all that chaos, the embarkation upon a great new adventure towards world efficiency. You, the motorists, are the chosen instruments of this revolution. By your united action, you can swiftly wrest power from the hands of inefficient, sentimental pedestrian cliques. Remember – your motor car is your weapon of victory. With it, you possess the means of triumphing over all opposition. Guard it carefully, use it ruthlessly, and victory is yours.

There followed precise details about meeting points at which motorists were to assemble, for dividing up into patrols and other small parties whose task would be to take over control of various public utilities and institutions. Motorists were to be allocated in most cases according to horsepower of their engines, but in certain instances according to the general structural design of their vehicle. Tourers and coupés were, in the main, to be directed to the country regions, where opposition was not expected to be concentrated or particularly violent. Saloons were massed for action in the cities, where their roofs and closed windows would offer some protection against isolated assaults. In the forefront of all such expeditions were to be double-decker omnibuses and six-wheel lorries, offering a fine barrage behind which the smaller cars could make their approach in comparative safety. Motoring oddities, like three-wheelers and jeeps, were to be used for special missions. So also were motor cycles, whose organisation had been placed under a special department. Secretly, they were looked on as expendable, suicide squads. It was hoped that most of them would be disposed of in accidents, natural or otherwise. At Burton's orders certain of the roadways on which they would travel had been covered with special greasy material to encourage skidding. In the new order of things, motor cars only were to be the standard vehicles of existence. Motor cycles were too individual, too flexible, and above all they represented independent action. It was a condition of membership of the League of Motorists that every motor car should be driven by two people, taking it in turns. Not only was this a popular measure, facilitating friendship and courtship, but it offered the League controllers greater opportunity of exercising authority – each driver being privately encouraged to keep a watchful eye upon his companion.

At mid-day, Burton made a quick survey of progress. It was very favourable. Special squads of supercharged racing cars had roared from one end of the country to another, with most efficient stops at key points to cut telephone wires and other communications. This had rendered all the easier the task of the main forces following in their wake. In each town the first task had been either the capture or destruction of all motors used in the service of local government officers and departments. Deprived of means of communication and transport, unable to consult with their colleagues or to give or receive orders of any kind, the authorities had offered very little resistance.

Strong motoring centres like Coventry and Birmingham were among the first to capitulate, owing to the presence of powerful partisan forces. Many aerodromes and aeroplane factories, too, came out in open support although Burton had, in any case, taken the precaution of diverting all petrol supplies, so that not a single aeroplane could leave the ground. In London the revolution was established with amazing efficiency. Using as bases a series of large garages situated in circular formation around the outskirts, Burton's forces penetrated in depth within half an hour, without encountering any opposition other than a few traffic lights and policemen. Policemen on point duty were inclined to be obstreperous, but fortunately the machine-minded car police swiftly grasped the immense possibilities of the new regime. Seeing that under it their function would be just the same, namely that of controlling and if necessary imprisoning opponents of the regime, they were able to be absorbed at once into the League's administrative framework.

By late afternoon it became evident that the League was winning the day, and with surprisingly little blood-shed. Almost without exception, all newspaper van drivers came over to the revolutionary party, and they at once distributed Burton's specially prepared propaganda sheets. Ordinary newspapers, on the other hand, were deprived of their usual distribution facilities. Faced with this insurmountable problem, and also the irresistible bait of reaching a new market of hundreds of thousands of motorists, one by one the newspaper owners fell into line with the new regime.

From then on the rout was complete. The League's shock squads occupied all Government departments and other official headquarters. Desperate last minute attempts to call out the Army were defeated by the same precaution as had grounded the Air Force – a complete stoppage of petrol supplies for any of the Army's lorries, tanks, armoured cars or other vehicles. Soon the League had taken over all broadcasting stations, to link up with the acquisition of that other moulder of public opinion, the Press.

At six o'clock Burton himself came to the microphone. He

spoke quietly, re-assuringly, yet with an underlying tone of authority which most listeners found impressive. He addressed himself first to the motorists, congratulating them on their great achievements in all parts of the country, urging on them eternal vigilance, and promising great new freedoms in the future. Provided they conformed with the League's forth-coming revised Motor Vehicle Regulations, they would have nothing to fear, he said. In return for their unquestioning obedience they could expect more petrol, more oil, cheaper tyres, abolition of traffic lights, improved garage services – and, very shortly, new cars to replace their old ones. It would be one of the League's first tasks, he said, to produce a standardised new car which would embody in one model all the latest improvements in car design, including self-changing gears, automatic steering, low vision windows, turnabout chairs, folding tables and unfolding camp beds. It was the League's ultimate intention to provide every motorist with a motor car which would give him all he needed in life – comfort, speed, leg-room, good vision, mechanical perfection and somewhere to sleep.

To the non-motorists Burton addressed himself briefly and somewhat evasively. He said that the best thing they could do was to remain at home and await a visit from their local MAO (Motor Administrative Officer). It would be for these officials to define whether or not pedestrians might ultimately qualify for a learner's course in driving, with a view to ultimate appointment to the ranks of LGLD (Low Grade Lorry Drivers). Burton did not elaborate on what prospect awaited pedestrians who were not so selected. In fact, even as he spoke, they were being rounded up all over the country by Motor Defence Buses, for imprisonment in a number of Displaced Pedestrians' Camps. From these they would, after a process of 'screening', either be sentenced to hard labour at one or other of the new motoring factories or – well, he hadn't quite had time to think what else to do with them. At the back of his mind was a project for using such abundant slave labour for the building of an immense Channel tunnel to connect up with Europe. But about that he must defer his decision until he was quite sure of the nature of Europe's reaction to the new revolution in Britain.

Europe's reaction was the inevitable one. A certain surprise at anything so dramatic as a revolution in Britain, but after that the usual admiration for the efficient way in which the British people dutifully 'set to' to make a success of any new form of government. Here and there enthusiastic groups of foreigners attempted to emulate Burton's revolution, but always the attempts failed through the individualistic nature of their approaches, coupled with disgraceful inefficiency. In France the attempt was foiled because it coincided with a Six Day Bicycle race, and most of the motorists parked their cars in order to watch the racing. In Holland one group of motorist revolutionaries did advance on Amsterdam, but it was tulip time and there was a flower fête and dancing in the streets, and altogether life did not encourage revolutions. In Spain a bullfight proved too great a counter attraction, while in Italy most of the motorists were too busy on the motor racing tracks. In Czechoslovakia there was considerable national sympathy with the motorist uprising, until an urgent directive was received from that exremely sympathetic neighbour, Russia, whereupon the Czechoslovak Ministry of the Interior arrested the ring leaders and held them for trial.

It was from Russia, in fact, that the new movement received its most vehement opposition, even to the extent of veiled threats of applying sanctions or, failing that, a few atomic bombs. Such an attitude surprised Burton, as he had assumed that in almost every way his system was identical with that of Soviet Russia. However, not to be outdone, he let it be known that Britain was producing a new motor car bomb that would outdo anything Russia had got. He also persuaded the American Government to stop exporting to Russia the latest Chevrolets, Studebakers, Chryslers, Cadillacs, Buicks and other American saloons and roadsters – a deprivation regarded by the Russians as far more serious than any wars or atom bombs.

At home the whole life of the nation had been re-organised,

efficiently, and as far as possible, quietly. What Glenser in one of his more inspired publicity phrases described as 'the motorisation of a nation' was progressing on several fronts at once. While factory production of cars was being speeded up a hundred and then two hundred per cent (naturally, rather at the expense of certain other products hitherto considered important – i.e. milk, bread, jam, sugar, clothes) an intensive testing of motorists' driving qualifications was going on all over the country. It was the League's ultimate intention to divide its membership into several grades, according largely to driving ability, although some allowances might have to be made for make and horse power of cars. The élite grade would consist of a hard core of drivers of racing cars, omnibuses, lorries, plus a few gifted individual drivers. This grade, Burton realised, would be united mainly by a hearty contempt for the inferior driving abilities of the next grade, and they by a similar contempt for the grade below them, and so on. It seemed to him an adequate system – vaguely reminiscent of a good many previous forms of government, of course – but far more efficient.

Meanwhile, at every school the curricula had been adapted so that students could be given a thorough grounding not only in the driving of motor cars, but in the whole process of mechanisation. Under the new regime, it became a condition of leaving school, or indeed of taking up any sort of occupation, that students should obtain their Motor Driving and Overhaul Certificate. The tests which they had to pass in order to obtain this certificate included driving at 90 miles an hour along the Kingston-Bypass, mending punctures without the necessary tools, and taking an engine completely to pieces and putting it together again in less than an hour.

The future for these boys and girls (there was no differentiation in the League's new state), offered several interesting prospects. They could go on to technical colleges and train to be lorry drivers or bus drivers, or they could pass on to universities and take their motor racing degrees (though here the standard was exceptionally high, and most rejects were such nervous wrecks that they were fit for nothing afterwards other than exile to the motor car factories). Then there were specialist courses in driving taxis, post office vans, steamrollers, tractors, etc.

For a time Burton was disturbed to notice an occasional tendency among the motoring population to 'drift'. Appointments began to be forgotten; drivers would actually stay at home rather than attend one of the National Car Rallies that were held in every district every week-end. It became necessary to send the motoring police and similar special services into action. Raids were made on the homes of suspect drivers, who were either warned and hustled on their way to the Rallies, or else arrested on the spot. Sometimes Burton decided it was necessary to make a public example of some recalcitrant motorist. On such occasions the unfortunate person and his companion were strapped into their car, which was set at the top of a steep hill, sprayed with petrol, the brakes loosened, and a match thrown into the bonnet as it began to career down the hill. What remained when the car hit the stone wall bend at the bottom of the hill was left on the spot as a permanent warning. After such examples, it was found that attendance of motorists at all State functions became 100 per cent.

In fact, in all ways the League of Motorists' revolution bid fair towards being one of the most successful and effective in all history. As the weeks, and then the months began to slip by, there was every excuse for Burton and his fellow leaders to sit back and pat themselves on the back. Britain was theirs, everywhere the motorist ruled, millions of miserable pedestrians slaved and hewed and hoed, and generally kept their masters.

Sad to relate, Burton was not afforded the pleasure of a well-earned relaxation. Slowly, but definitely, evidence began to accumulate that there was opposition within the realm – an underground movement at work. Leaflets were found scattered in the streets, in the post, inside motor car factories. Slogans and insults to the regime appeared on hoardings, or chalked across walls and doorways. Try as they might, the motorised police failed to get on the track of the resistance. And so, in the nature of things, its importance began to grow through the legend of its mystery.

Where Burton made his mistake was in assuming that any resistance must in fact, be coming from within the ranks of the motorists themselves. It is, of course, a pardonable weakness of all who assume absolute power that its alarming potentialities breeds in them a growing distrust of all around them, notably their closest associates. Soon Burton distrusted everyone, from the Chief of the Motorised Police to such intimates as Glenser. He even, unhappily, began to wonder about his own wife, and every time she ran into the town in her white coupé to do some shopping, he had her followed by a nondescript black saloon in which were two of the smartest trailers in the motorised police. Later, as a further precaution, Burton employed a secret service motor man to follow the police.

But the trouble came from a source quite unsuspected. At the time of the revolution some of Burton's associates had recommended destroying the railway services, just as the aeroplane services were destroyed (their parts came in useful for making new cars). Burton had decided against this, however, judging rightly that there would inevitably be a need for some large scale means of transporting goods and pedestrians to various parts of the country. At that time he did not feel so sure of his position that he liked to risk placing large quantities of pedestrians into motor lorries and omnibuses, with the possibility of their overpowering the drivers and staging a revolt. So, while withdrawing three-quarters of the railway engines and carriages from service, he had ordered the running of routine services of trains between the main towns and cities.

In order to operate the trains, it had been necessary to retain the services of a number of drivers, firemen, engineers and maintenance men – though, of course, strict orders had gone out that they were to receive special courses in political re-education. Unfortunately these courses could not have been strict enough, and it was a group of railway executives and drivers who had secretly got together to organise the new underground movement. Though lacking an individual leader of the brilliance of Burton, they numbered among their fellows at least a dozen first-class technical brains, including the man who evolved the British railway time-table, the man who used to drive the Royal Train, the man who ran Crewe signal box for ten years, and the head of the goods department at one of the big London stations. These men, between them, concocted a plan to overthrow and defeat the League of Motorists, basing it on an efficient use of railway engines and stock. At all depots maintenance men were sworn to keep their engines in the peak of condition. Shunters and linesmen and signal box men, even dining car attendants – all came into the scheme. Secret supplies of coal were carried about in goods vans outwardly appearing to contain motor car tyres and petrol cans. The final contact was with a group of frustrated Army locomotion engineers who managed to arrange a supply of machine guns, rifles, and mounted guns.

Where Burton's revolution was organised in a blaze of publicity, the railway revolution was developed under a cloak of complete secrecy. When it finally broke it came as a complete shock to the motorists – partly, of course, because the day cunningly chosen was that of the weekly National Car Rallies, when all motorists were gathered at a set number of stadiums and centres. This suited the railway rebels admirably. During the previous night normal time-tables had been scrapped, and by the middle of the day not only the usual trains, but some one thousand extra trains were on the lines. They steamed into every city, into every town, and along every branch and sub-branch line. Each one pulled at least a dozen carriages, whose body work had been stripped down to accommodate guns, ammunition and several hundreds of armed rebels. Most of the carriages had been covered with armour plating.

It was perhaps not such a bloodless revolution, but at least the bloodshed was concentrated. Heavy artillery fire was directed on each of the Car Rallies, and within a few minutes motorists were scattering in confusion. Subsidiary forces landed fire bombs on the car factories, burning them all to the ground. Such resistance as could be mobilised was almost ineffective, for it is difficult to hit a moving object, and all trains had strict orders to keep puffing.

In one day, as opposed to Burton's five, the Railway Rebels had acquired power. At once a meeting was held at Euston Station and a British Railway Government was set up. The country was divided into areas, each under a Railway Executive Officer. All motor cars were destroyed, and the public issued with instructions that travel was forbidden except by railway. The leaders of the League of Motorists, excepting Glenser, who joined the Railway Rebels as Director of Publicity, and Burton, who had fled with his wife to America in the one remaining passenger aircraft that he had thoughtfully secreted in his back garden, were bound and gagged and placed aboard a small express train. The brakes were removed, full steam pressure engaged, and the engine set in motion along a desolate branch track near the Cornish coastline. As the track came to an end down a steep hill facing a short run of grass sloping down to cliffs and a drop of several hundred feet, and as the buffers of the terminus had been removed, we need not dwell further on the fate of the leaders of the League of Motorists. Perhaps it was consolation to them in their last moments to reflect that at some date in the future statues would be erected to their memory, and their behaviour fitted into the current history books of the day, according to which party was in power.

Meanwhile, life went on, Glenser excelled himself in publicising the British Railway System, symbol of all that was good and fine in mankind. Every infant that was born in the new state was presented with a box containing a toy engine and railway lines, so that he should develop, from an early age, the right mentality for fitting into a railway state. All reference to motor cars were erased from books, magazines, films, theatres, and all garages and petrol pumps were removed and sold to Middle East States who were still backward enough to rely on motor cars. Once again school curricula were changed round, once again people were graded into classes, once again the system of society was organised on a footing strangely remininscent of the past – but, of course, more efficient.

Alas, sad to relate, the Railway Rebels, too, found it difficult to relax. Slowly but definitely, evidence began to accumulate that there was opposition within the realm. Leaflets were found scattered in the corridors of railway trains, inside engine sheds, under the domes of big stations. Slogans and insults to the regime appeared on the doors of railway carriages, over the windows of refreshment rooms, up and down moving stairways. Try as they would, the railway police failed to get on the track of the resistance. And so, in the nature of things, its importance began to grow through the legend of its mystery.

Where the Railway Rebels made their mistake was in assuming that any resistance must come from within the ranks of their own members. For, as a matter of fact, there were still a few pedestrians alive. They were men and women of no power whatsoever, knowing little about motor cars and still less about railway engines, having precious little desire to travel at all – wanting merely to live their lives without offence. They were so illiterate and dull-witted that they could not comprehend how vitally important it was that petrol should be available, that tyres should be cheap, that new jet-propelled railway engines should travel from London to Edinburgh in half the time they used to do so. They clung to an obstinate, uneducated sort of idea – which they were clumsy at expressing – that there was life before machines, that perhaps there would still be life long after the machines had destroyed themselves.

And so, all over the country, forming haphazard, muddled but defiant little cells, these pedestrians began making their own revolution. They lacked all ideas for organisation and efficiency. They omitted to build up stores of rifles and ammunition. They forgot to divert supplies of petrol and to amass quantities of coal. They could not be bothered to alter time-tables nor to arrange car rallies. They had no money to spend on propogating a cause, even if they were sure they had a cause to propagate. They made no attempt to exercise authority over their fellows, nor to abuse their rights of property. In fact they made no change in their ways of living at all, continuing to love one another, to help one another and to serve the common good – a life which, by example, began to impress people very much.

This, of course, was the most dangerous revolutionary movement that could possibly be imagined. The Railway Rebels – like the League of Motorist or any other single-minded government – took steps to crush it completely.

The most we can hope for is that they have not yet succeeded.

XI

Dance of the Drum

The drum was thick and round, curved into the shape of a woman's thigh. The dark-stained wood was polished and streaky, and the skin pulled taut over the hollow and, shone with a faint, eerie light of its own, like some evil winking eye. It lay bright and gleaming across the bare brown legs of the squatting drummer, a small, knobbly-limbed old man with hollow eyes and a bleak bald head. His thin arms threshed the air wildly, the bony fingers making darted feints towards the sweat glistening on his high forehead, he lowered his hands, sweeping them in long, delicate strokes above the shining drum-face. Dropping lower and lower, lower and lower; suddenly, in a swift, savage movement, jabbing a long, crooked finger downwards.

The first beat of the drum shattered the stillness of the night into a thousand fragmentary echoes, rumbling over the bowed black heads of the expectant crowd, quivering through the long lines of brown-skinned dancers. At its beckoning sound the dancers, poised statue-like around the flickering, newly-lit fire, became alive, throwing back their thick-cropped heads, writhing into movement. They began to move slowly around the circle of the fire, the flames from the fire lighting up their naked bodies, covered with vivid daubs of crimson. As they moved in and out of the firelight the paint began to melt, oozing and trickling across the twisting limbs until the bodies, already gleaming with sweat, had the appearance of being wound about with hundreds of coiled snakes.

The drummer sat high above the dancers, half in shadow, the light falling emphatically on the drum, so that the only parts of him that mattered were his long arms, curving like claws above the drum-face. His hands began beating into the hard, tight skin of the drum, the movements jagged and staccato, as if impelled by some strange magnetic force from within the drum rather than by any effort of the man himself. The strange flat sounds thudded out into the night, extending their convulsive hypnotism to the dancers. As if obeying a command, they began moving in a swaying chain away from the fire, towards the wailing drum. They gathered in a fan-shape around the drummer, eyes closed, thick lips frothing and protruding, bodies thrown forward, arms outstretched pleadingly, as if abandoning themselves completely to the peremptory control of the drum.

Slowly the drum thumped out its story. At the first sharp beat the shining bodies twisted up, merging into the air, and at the second beat they obediently crashed down, their feet shuddering the soft earth. Then the drummer's fingers rolled across the wide drum-face, pouring thunder into the air, and at the sound the dancers began to writhe backwards and forwards, clutching at each other's whirling limbs, twisting into the shape of a winding brown snake. Suddenly the beat of the drum crashed into silence; and from far away came a low chanting. It grew louder and louder, swelling up out of the darkness, swaying nearer and nearer to the arena.

A great line of brown figures appeared, forming in a circle around the fire. The chanting ceased; a shrill voice carried out an order; from out of the darkness something hurtled, as if thrown by many hands, rolling over and over along the ground until it came to a stop under the shadow of the drummer. Slowly, painfully the shape uncoiled, stretched out, half-raised to a crouching obeisance. The slender figure of a girl, her thick brown limbs tinged with a strange ethereal whiteness, and softly and delicately outlined against the firelight.

The swift thump of the drum broke out again, harshly splitting the silence. This time it had a new note, a quicker tempo, the sudden pitter-patter of fingers drumming out a long pent-up excitment, echoing like rain on the roof-tops.

The sound of the drum swept along, whirling all sounds, all unspoken cried and unsung songs, into a single sound, into its own dull, ominous rumbling. At its angry command, as though startled out of a dream, the crouching girl sprang to her feet. She whirled round and round, then transfixed into a brown marble statue: staring up towards the drum, awaiting the next crashing thunder, while a bloodless finger poised. For a moment the girl remained there, offering herself up as the dancers had done, offering up her gleaming face, her glaring eyes, her curved, straining body; her firm, rounded breasts thrust up towards the echoing drum, her swaying hands outstretched in a queer gesture of pleading and surrender. The the crusted finger-balls bounced on to the skin, the drum beat its relentless message. The girl threw back her head and whirled into a wild dance.

The dancers, with a swift movement, had formed a circle around the girl. Within this small space she now began to dance, while the dancers swayed in and out. As she danced her arms and legs moved in queer staccato thrusts, in time to the beat of the drum. At first the movement was steady, almost rhythmic, then, imperceptibly, the drumming became sharper, more jagged, so that the girl writhed and twisted in the effort to keep time. Within a few moments her body was bathed in sweat … But the drum went on faster and faster, singing out its quickening message under the beat of the tireless fingers, and the girl danced faster and faster. Her eyes closed and she seemed to render up the last vestige of her personality, becoming completely a possession of the drum, a part of the very drumming itself. She danced in the small circle of earth where she had first fallen, churning up the soil around her into a wild froth, her sleek limbs whirring and hissing through the air in their endless, helpless movements. And as she danced the long brown snake of the other dancers curved and coiled around her, always swaying a little closer, the circle becoming smaller, the walls moving nearer.

Now there was no end and no beginning to the sound of the drum; it became an endless rumble, like the water falling over stones, like the thunder tumbling through the skies, like the surging, beating heart of the deep earth. The drum-face shone brighter and brighter, polished by the stroking of the drummer's fingers. Sometimes it was coloured bright red with blood from the flaked finger-tips, but still the drumming went on, the long rolling beat of the drum. All around there was silence, not the murmur of a child, nor the wail of a mother, nor the war-cry of a warrior, only the heavy silence, drowned under the drumming. Slowly the rhythm mounted to a savage, compelling crescendo, and the girl's dancing became more frenzied. She hurled herself into the air, tearing at her straggling hair, clutching at her pointed, trembling breasts. She span round wildly; once, twice, a third time. Then she fell back exhausted into the arms of the waiting dancers.

The drum thumped out its inexorable demands. Obediently the dancers broke into movement. The leaders seized the girl, lifting her high above them, so that she was silhouetted against the firelight: the dangling limbs, the heaving breasts, the drooping hair; the sweat dripping slowly and finally into the dry, dusty ground. Then, as the drum boomed on, louder and faster than ever before (the sudden torrent of words), the dancers leapt into action, began running away from the drum and towards the fire and the sky-high flames. With swift movements four of them gripped the legs and arms of the girl, swung her down to the ground and then, with a swelling of glittering muscles, hurled her high up into the air. Momentarily the body disappeared, lost in the hanging night sky. Then it came tumbling down out of the lost darkness, writhing and twisting like some strange shining spear ... diving remorselessly into the glowing heart of the fire, sending showers of sparks over the dancers.

For a moment the drum broke its throbbing, the air hushed, the dancers froze into monuments, the flames flickered low. In that moment a faint wailing sprang from some faraway hidden depth of the surrounding darkness. It rose and fell tremulously, a reed-like, inconsolable sound, sadder and fainter than the solitary cry of an animal for its mate. Then it was smashed out of hearing by a decisive thud of the drum, the signal for a thousand voices to howl out their vast, triumphant shriek of achievement, the proud, lusting call of fulfilment.

The voices sang and screamed until they were hoarse, the dancers writhed and twisted until they fell in crumpled heaps to the ground, but the thud-thud-thud of the drum went on and on and on. The tireless fingers clawed across the drum-face, the rumbling of the drum filled the air, echoed into the night, drowning all voices and all sounds. The rumble, rumble, rumble of the drum, spinning from tree-top to tree-top, shivering the lonely leaves, creasing the quiet surfaces of the lakes, thudding deep into the rocky heart of the earth. The polished drum with the shining skin. And the fresh red blood-spots.

XII

Justice of the Sea

Hendrikson had set his heart on the boat. There were several good reasons: freedom, a home, a profitable means of business – to put it more bluntly, smuggling. But there was something beyond that, connected with his childhood at Rotterdam and how he used to sit on the harbour wall and watch the squat fishing boats as they smacked into the teeth of white waves on their way out to the North Sea. These snub-nosed Boeiers with their graceful swelling lines, their tall masts, their huge red sails – he had never forgotten them.

And now far from home, here at a Thames-side mooring on the outer environs of London, he had come across one of these old Boeiers. Old perhaps though not as they went, built by van Duijvendijk at Lekkerker about 1910 but still a sight for any Dutchman's eyes. He couldn't wait until he met the owner, a small tight faced wizened old man with sharp and rather unfriendly eyes. And that was when the trouble began …

Hendrikson tried hard to be friendly but the old man seemed aloof. At last he came out in the open and said, 'Look, I'd like to buy your boat,' though in reality he hadn't the least idea how to raise the money.

It was the only time he was ever to see a smile on the old man's face. A wintry, mirthless and mocking smile.

'Hendrikson,' said the old man grimly. 'This boat's not for the likes of you.'

Somehow that made Hendrikson see red. He was almost blind with his anger against Ramsden. And somehow he couldn't leave it alone. Day after day the big burly Dutchman would hang around the riverside, looking with brooding eyes across at the boat which had become a centre of his life. For he could not help thinking of all those things he could do, running her over to Holland, and back, picking up a nice load of contraband each time. He knew all the tricks. He had contacts.

At first he thought of stealing the boat. But he knew that wouldn't be enough. The old man would raise a hue and cry.

But if the old man wasn't there to raise a hue and cry.

Hendrikson knew he had the answer. Ramsden was a solitary old devil, he didn't seem to have any relatives, or indeed any real friends. If the boat went off one day and never came back, no one would be any wiser. So long as Ramsden himself wasn't left behind to raise any objections.

Hendrikson knew the old man's habits. He knew that every Saturday night he spent the evening at a nearby riverside pub, returning usually about midnight. More often than not he was a bit fuzzy with drink. He wouldn't be in any condition to offer any opposition.

Nor, when the time came, was he. Hendrikson hid behind the top of the companion way, and when the old man's swaying figure had started to climb awkwardly down – he leaped forward and gave him a ferocious shove. With a clatter and rattle, Ramsden fell head over heels and sprawled awkwardly on to the saloon floor.

Hendrikson could never be quite sure whether he meant to kill the old man. He supposed there would really have been no alternative, sooner or later. Anyway, the point became unimportant, for when he climbed down to inspect, he found Ramsden had broken his neck, and was very, very dead.

Now that he was committed, Hendrikson wasted no tears. With an effort – the old man was surprisingly heavy for his appearance – he dragged the body over to the settee, and laid him out there, covering him with a blanket. There would be time to dispose of him later on, when they were out at sea. Now the immediate problem was to get everything ready so that the boat could slip away with the early morning tide.

For several hours Hendrikson went about his work, quietly

stowing things away and getting the barge ready for her voyage. Just as dawn was threatening on the eastern horizon he unfurled the big mainsail, cast off the lines, and the big Boeier glided out into mid-stream; heeling slightly, she began to sail down the broad River Thames towards the estuary mouth, her small white dinghy trailing neatly behind on a rope.

At first Hendrikson felt nervous: it was a long time since he had stood on the deck of a Boeier, even longer since he had held one of the great thick tillers in his arms.

But as time passed, and the boat sailed on – down past Gravesend and Greenwich, and out by the great Nore – ahead all the wide open spaces of the North Sea – Hendrikson felt able to relax. He began to think about his gruesome cargo below, the crumpled figure of the old man, wondering when it would be safe to consign him to the safe oblivion of the sea.

So engrossed was he in his thoughts, that he did not really take much heed of the sky behind him, now colouring an ominous dark. Perhaps he would have noticed the first vicious jerks of the on-coming wind, were it not for a more immediate, and shocking moment. For even as he watched, the two doorways of the companion head suddenly seemed to whip open.

Involuntarily, the big Dutchman gave a scream, and let go the tiller. The very next moment the doors whipped back again, and a part of him recognised that the wind had been responsible for the apparently supernatural incident.

But by then it was too late. Swinging free the tiller came round, the boat faltered, the oncoming wind caught smack at the mainsail – and with a crack like a whip the boom swung over.

Hendrikson had no chance to save himself. The boom caught him in the chest and sent him hurtling over the side into the sea. Within a few seconds he was floundering in the water while the barge ploughed on into the waves. And then, almost hitting him, there came surging the little white dinghy.

Threshing the water Hendrikson managed to grab the side of the dinghy. Half awash with sea he managed to pull himself up until at last he fell exhausted aboard. There he lay, helpless, like a drowned rat, unable to move, moaning slightly, as with eyes still capable of observing he watched the great mast of the Boeier swirling on into the wind as it carried forward this strangest of cargoes.

It was about ten minutes later and he was still too weak to do more than stare, helplessly, when a Medway fishing boat came by and, observing his plight, threw a line aboard the Boeier.

'Don't worry, mate,' called out one of the fishermen cheerfully, 'We'll just get your boat under control and then we'll put you aboard.'

But when they emerged from the saloon of the Boeier, fresh with the horror of their discovery, they looked back – and saw that the white dinghy was once again empty.

XIII

A Lift to London

He gave me a lift one Sunday morning. I was hitching to London. I'd walked three miles out of Exeter. It was eight o'clock in the morning, not the sort of time to expect a lift really.

I heard a car whining softly up the incline. It purred to a stop – a long, sleek roomy saloon – and there he was leaning across the seat, a stout round-faced man, middle-aged, with a wrinkled forehead.

'Want a lift?'

I got in and sank gratefully into the seat beside him. It was like floating on air.

Beside me the driver sat comfortably, his stoutness firmly planted in the seat, his short tubby legs lying easily in front. One foot rested on the accelerator, the other tapped the footboards. He drove with apparent casualness, caressing the broad steering wheel with two fingers, leaning his other arm on the window sill, head tilted to one side, brim of a thick felt hat shading his eyes. He seemed to pay little attention to the grey moving ribbon of the road – yet somehow his driving held a touch of confidence ... part of a subtle air of authority reflected by the limousine, his expensive clothing, the thin gold watch on his wrist, the polish of his clean well kept hands ...

'Going far?' he said after a while.

I looked at him half apologetically.

'Well, as a matter of fact, I'm hoping to make London.'

He slanted his eyes towards me. They were large, round eyes ... Meeting them I was surprised to see that they were strangely fixed and glassy, cloaked by a film of vacancy, as if they were not really seeing anything.

'London?' He repeated the name, rolling it round his tongue as if he had some difficulty in fixing it into the new blankness of his mind. Then it seemed to register, and a vague smile twisted his lips.

'You're lucky then. I'm going nearly that far, I can drop you not more than half an hour away.'

I thanked him profusely, but before I could think of anything further to say that would prolong the conversation he relapsed into silence again.

We drove on, floating effortlessly over lonely roads, keeping up a steady 50 miles an hour. Now and then, when he was staring ahead, I studied him out of the corner of my eye.

I guessed at his age – say 50 – and at his occupation – say rich and successful company director. I wondered where he came from and where he was going. I could not help feeling envy at his richness and comfort, his evident all-round prosperity. I reflected with some sort of bitterness that if you had the money you could do anything, even these inflated days, including driving a luxury car to London.

Then I noticed the tired sagging of his red-flecked cheeks, the surprising dark rims under his eyes – above all the queer lost look in his face – and I realised with a sense of shame that I knew no more about him than I did about the blurred Sunday gardener we had just swept past in the previous village.

Sitting there, watching his round flabby chin drooping into the rough collar of his coat, I, too, began to feel the weight of some inexorable burden that lay painfully across the burly shoulders beside me.

No doubt he sensed my curiosity. Several times he cast a weak half smile at me, a smile that may have been intended to apologise, to explain, but that only succeeded in conveying to me something of the hidden pain of his thoughts.

Suddenly we began passing the flat lines of an aerodrome: there was a glimpse of drawn-up fighters, the blur of a hangar. A few figures in RAF blue were on the road, some of them thumbing hopefully for a lift. Rather to my surprise, instead of slowing down he pressed his foot hard on the accelerator, shooting the big car foward like a bullet.

I looked at him more closely. His eyes had gone dull again. He did not speak for several moments, then turned to me.

'Air Force lads, eh?'

I said, 'Yes,' not knowing what else to say, feeling that in some way I could not comprehend a wound buried deep within him, far beneath his protective veneer of stout luxury, had been cut open suddenly as if by a surgeon's impartial knife.

We went on, through Salisbury, on towards Basingstoke, on and on towards the distant environs of London. At last the big car slackened speed and we drew up, silently and smoothly, along a wide stretch of open road.

'I'll have to drop you here,' he said.

I reached for my rucksack, and then turned towards him.

'Well, I certainly am very much obliged – '

The rest of my words stuck in my throat. Instead of saying any more he had turned and looked full at me. His eyes were no longer without expression, they were wide and round, like a child's – and glittering with unshed tears. When suddenly he began speaking it was as if the words could not come out fast enough.

'My son's in the RAF. you know. Very clever, too – passed out with full honours. Commissioned and all that. Everyone thinks the world of him, they say he'll be a top ranking officer one day.'

He paused, curiously: and then went on, forcing out the gulping, awkward words.

'I'm on my way to his aerodrome now. I had a wire this morning from the Air Ministry. There's been an accident ... a crash ... They say that there are – no survivors.'

The words rang out cold and metallic, hanging in the silent air like drawn daggers, merging into the dull endless throb of the engine, sinking like time-bombs into the satin-covered cushions.

I couldn't say anything. I got out of the car and shut the door. Through the glass window I saw his face, wide open with sudden apprehension, his eyes pleading to be shielded from what they must soon see. For a moment I endured his gaze helplessly, then I averted my eyes and stood back.

I watched while he revved up the engine and let in the clutch. The car moved forward slowly, majestically. Its shining body curved away from me, gracefully following a bend ... soon the black luxurious shape had disappeared sleekly into the distance, the purring engine fading into an echo.

Turning, I began walking along the road. I walked a mile before a London bound furniture van picked me up – and even then the driver had to call out three times before I heard him offering me a lift.

XIV

A Day to Remember

He woke up full to the brim with the strangest feeling. He, Alfred, wizened, humped-up, short-sighted, white-haired, sniffly, slovenly, lonely and unloved, sad and socially useless old man, was going to die.

This day, this very new and fresh and sweet and promising day, full of all manner of hopes and sunshine: he was going to pass out of it like a departing shadow.

It was an awful, heavy feeling. The old man liked it so little that he hastened to wake up, shaking his head, sniffing, coughing, perhaps shivering – then telling himself, it was only a dream, really, only a dream.

But what a strange thing to dream. Why should an old and tired man in his seventieth year have a dream like that? He shook his white head rather doubtfully, rather uneasily, and climbed out of bed, and, in his slow and tottery way, dressed himself.

He couldn't forget it, either. He crouched over his little gas ring boiling a kettle, then he made the tea and sat with both gnarled hands clutching the steaming cup, and as he sipped the warm liquid gratefully between dry old lips his mind was darting back all the time. Strange sort of dream to have, don't you think? For an old, old man like Alfred.

He wasn't exactly frightened. Disturbed, that was more like it. It set you thinking, somehow. And an old fellow with white hairs and nigh on seventy years of back life to review – well, he had a lot to think on.

And it wasn't too good that was the trouble. Where had he gone? What had he achieved? What was he doing alone and unwanted, leaving no trace at all in this bed-sitting room?

He tut-tutted, rose with some difficulty and went to stand in front of the cracked mirror. Was this him then – Alfred? Why wasn't it Sir Alfred? or – well almost anything but plain Alfred. What about the companies he might have led, the houses he might have owned, the luxuries he might have enjoyed – what about the wife and the children and the grandchildren?

Two facing, light-blue watery eyes came near to shedding a tear. True it was self-pity and all that: but it was sad. Sad old Alfred who had never married, never begot his children, never really done anything.

He pursued the elusive morning, still haunted by his dream. But memory was kind to him, faded a little, softened a little: by the time he took his morning stroll in the park, the darker side of it had dwindled.

But the disturbance remained. It was a little like indigestion; irritating, hanging about, not to be fobbed off – so that when he sat himself heavily in the park seat and poked with his walking stick at the leaves – he was poking at all the memories of his life, as each one arose and annoyed him. Silly old fool, Alfred! Why did you do that? And why *didn't* you do that? And what about – what about – ?

There the old head might have nodded, the nostrils dilated and taken a deep breath, there the morning nap might have taken charge. But not this morning. There was a sort of restlessness, a lack of content. Plopping and pouting his old lips, Alfred struggled to his feet and stumped off along the footpath leaning heavily on his stick – like a man embarking on some journey that had no purpose, and yet had.

And all the time, as he stumped along, he thought with disgust and distaste of the seventy years he had wasted – no other word. Why hadn't he – why hadn't he – but in vain he tried to grasp at the disappearing castles in the air. He hunched up his shoulders and stared at the ground and walked on. He *hadn't*, that was the trouble. He just hadn't. He might as well – might as well never have lived.

He came to the bridge over the lake, where the ducks swam in lazy circles. He leaned over this, glad of the rest, for he was

quickly tired these days. He stared into the water and saw
reflected the graceful line of the bridge, the dark blob of himself,
the vast sky behind – infinitesimal, that was what he was. Who
would care, know worry, think twice when he was gone?

He coughed, a wheezy old sound, and turned to lean back and
stare across the park. That dream now, that strange dream –
what had it been about? Strange, strange ... Everything when
you came to think about it, was strange. But that dream: well
now, he couldn't even remember it. But it was something –
something –

With a shrug the old man turned off the bridge. And as he
moved, one tired eye caught an odd blob of colour. He didn't
know quite what was odd about it; but despite his seventy
ancient years some deep instinct stirred in those dried veins and
prompted him to look round, more carefully, at the flash of
colour.

And at once he saw what was wrong. It was almost like a scene
from a film. There was a pram, a large black pram, and sitting
up in the pram was the bright blob of colour, a little boy with a
red jersey and bright red beret, looking across to where some
few yards away his nurse was talking to a friend.

And what was wrong, what was terribly wrong, was that the
blob of colour was moving. Across the golden morning, past the
fresh green background, the pram was moving with ever-
increasing speed – moving down the slope of smooth grass that
led straight to the edge of the lake.

It was one of those terrible, inevitable sequences of events, the
nurse turning away, the brake perhaps slipping, the pram on a
slope, the bright baby swishing towards the waiting dark waters.

The nurse had turned too late, was gesticulating. The baby
had started, aware of the vanishing world to scream. And an old
white-haired man had begun running ...

He never knew the facts of the matter. He saw only the
dwindling space between the pram and the water, the stretch of
green, green grass over which a miracle must hurtle his tired old
body – fast, fast, faster than the hounds of heaven, faster than
time itself.

He was conscious, vaguely, of his pounding feet, the soft

ground scrunching, the wind against his cheeks. In the urgency of the action he had forgotten to breathe; now, suddenly, appallingly, he had to heave in great throbbing gasps. He felt the throbbing, the beating of his heart, the rising darkness like waves of the sea – but his bleary, bloodshot staring old eyes saw that pram, a yard or two at the most from the precipice of a baby's life.

And with a wild, clumsy, tumbling-over, but effective lunge forward Alfred threw his seventy years of hope and memories down in front of the sedate black pram, grasping at it with resolute arms as it hurtled forward, holding it for that precious moment of impact, jolting it to a stop before the seas broke over, the sky fell in, and the merciful, dreamed-of darkness came with its blessed peace.

'The poor, brave old man,' they said, gathering in a quick crowd. The nurse wept tears, and tenderly wiped blood from a scratch on his head before folding the lifeless old arms piously across the silent chest. She would never forget, she swore, never, never forget the brave old man. And the crowd, moved with pity, agreed, and someone went off to telephone the newspapers so that others should know, and never forget.

But the bright blob of red in the pram, reassured, lay kicking and gurgling and staring with wonder at the vast blue sky, the golden sun, the promise of life's glories to come. And that – *that* was the best of all reasons to make it a day to remember.

XV

The Face in the Window

Walking round the bend into Station Road John Foster automatically looked up at the house on the corner. As his gaze travelled over the austere pattern of Victorian windows a faint smile hovered at his lips. He smiled because he was remembering the first time he had looked up. Then it had been by the merest chance, his mind had been far away – only to be jogged back to reality by the shock, the quick stab of half-recognition.

But during the days and weeks since it was no mere chance that sent his gaze sweeping sideways – no mere chance but an intensity of purpose, without whose attainment he would have been miserable. What might have been no more than a morning incident had grown out of all proportion, so that now it was the most significant moment of his day. Beside it the rest – work at the office, lunch with friends, evenings with his wife and children – seemed faded and almost unreal. Without it ... but no, he could not bear to imagine.

And now his gaze fell on the big first-floor bay window, and his search was ended. The smile at his lips burst into fruition, lighting up his whole face, and his eyes beamed brightly as they saw – perhaps for the twentieth time, yet in some way always for the first time – the woman at the window.

She was as anonymous to him as that, yet he felt he knew her more closely, more intimately, than – well, sometimes he had dared the comparison, than his own wife. When he had first seen her, sitting at the window, as cool and composed, and beautifully detached as any of the statues and portraits one sometimes saw posed in windows, he had not been able to think coherently, to say to himself, oh, yes, there is a pretty woman, or how lovely she looks framed in the window. It had not been like that at all – just a blind wave, an impulse, taking hold of him. A sense of knowledge, of secret and mysterious acquaintance. For a second their eyes had met and in that second he could have sworn there was some communication between them.

Or perhaps he imagined it all? At first he tried to tell himself that, he even tried to pretend to believe it. But each day, as his steps took him nearer to the corner, all the doubts fell away from him: he could only think with suppressed excitement, *in half a minute I shall see her – after another twenty steps I will look up and our eyes will meet and I will know again that exquisite eternal moment.* And when at last the moment was there and his gaze found hers she seemed touched into life. Her dark eyes pulled at him with mysterious strength, her face was animated, the lips parted, the high cheekbones flushed, there was a sudden ripple of whiteness as she curved her neck to look down. Oh, God, she was as lovely as a Rembrandt painting, framed there in some old Victorian window with her red-gold hair a perfect background to the simple loveliness of her face.

So lovely, in her remote way, that John Foster could seldom get the image out of his mind. He began to take her with him on his journeys. She stood near his desk at work, she sat at the next table at lunch, she hovered dangerously around the placid life of his home in the suburbs. Sometimes, indeed, her presence seemed so real that he was afraid his wife, Olive, would surely notice. But no, she didn't. She was too placid and settled, it would never have occurred to her that another woman might intrude into the cosiness of their existence.

When he found himself thinking like that he would hate the disloyalty. Hadn't he been married happily for several years? Hadn't he two adorable children, a sweet and devoted wife, a warm, pleasant home? … Yes, all those things he could tabulate. But against them loomed this single image, this worrying outline of what might-have-been, or perhaps even – what-might-be.

Every morning that he approached the corner his mind played with the dangerous concept. Every morning he was not really walking to catch the 8.40 train, but marching into the excitement of a new future. He could not help himself! As he walked along the succession of dreamlike conjectural images floated through his mind. The secret meeting, the long train journey into the unknown, perhaps somewhere a boat, too – the emergence into some completely different world, tropical seas, exotic colours, languorous nights. And always with him at his side – in his arms, warm and throbbing – there was this woman, this half-real, half-imagined woman upon whom he gazed with such passion and ardour every morning at about 8.36 a.m.

Yes, it had come to that. It was already a form of disloyalty. He could no longer kiss Olive goodbye in the mornings without a sense of shame, of unworthiness; as if, already, he was taking leave of his wife to visit a mistress. But no, it could never be like that, he knew. The very furtiveness would be too much. It would have to be one thing or another, the old life or the new. And at the thought of all the pain and suffering such a choice must occasion he would feel miserable, quite ill. And yet ...

And yet, when he looked at the window and saw the woman, he forgot all about such thoughts. He forgot everything but himself – himself and this woman, whom he knew and yet did not know, whom he desired and yet was half afraid of. Who was she? What did she do? Was she married? Had she children? Strange, but none of these thoughts bothered him. Their relationship was as simple as that, or so he liked to think. External things did not matter. All that mattered was the look that passed between them, the language of their eyes, of temptation, of their future together ...

And thinking thus, on this particular morning, he knew that things could not go on as they were. He could not go on living in this tortured way, caught between two worlds. He saw himself at a crossroads, compelled to take a step one way or another. He saw the need either to sacrifice his wife and family, his home and his familiar life – or that lovely inscrutable image which shone like a beckoning flame. And like many men before him he looked doggedly, a little desperately, towards the flame, as if determined to stare at its brightness until he was blinded to all else.

That morning as he walked round the corner his footsteps slackened, and when he came to the gateway to the house he stopped. He was still looking up at the window, still looking into the woman's eyes. Now he tried to communicate his intentions, tried to signal the meaning of this terribly important break in the pattern. He thought, but could not be sure, that she understood. Then he opened the gate and walked up towards the porch.

Curiously, the walk seemed an extraordinarily long one. His feet seemed heavy and clumsy; he almost had to force them forward. And as he did so the nerves of his body tingled all over and he felt – well, frightened, almost fearful. For the very opening of the gate, the very embarkation on that walk, seemed to split his life to its foundations. He had a mental picture of Olive at home, washing the breakfast things, of his baby daughter sleeping in her pram in the garden; of his young son now at the day school shuffling into place for the morning prayers. He saw these threads of his life spinning out in their different directions ... and then, as if they had been reeled in again, he caught a picture of the family together again, sitting in the evening round the supper table; the meal over and Olive reading the evening paper while he sat back and smoked a pipe and surveyed his two children.

John Foster's footsteps faltered. How strange that there should be this vivid memory at this moment. And he remembered, he could not help it, the legend about the drowning man whose life passes before his eyes in a moment, even as he is about to lose it.

He found himself standing at the porch. The door inside was open and he had a glimpse into a shadowy hallway. Without thinking much his eyes took in the old-fashioned hall-stand with brass rings; from it hung a woman's coat, some children's macintoshes, and a man's overcoat and hat.

For a moment John Foster stared upon this scene as if the stage properties took a few seconds to register on his confused mind. And indeed he could never be clear whether they did, for in all honesty he was not thinking of the revelatory world of children and a man's coat and hat, but of his own – his own precious, vivid world, which had grown up *inside*, and not outside, his lifetime. Suddenly he did not want to lose it, suddenly it was important – so important that he almost cried before the wonder of all that he possessed.

And with that thought, he turned and hurried away down the path. At the gate he paused and half turned back, looking upward to where the woman sat at the window. With a sudden gesture, he raised his hat and smiled, almost apologetically. In some way, he thought, perhaps she understood: for her smile back was tinged with sadness.

And then he closed the gate and sprinted down the road towards the station. By a stroke of luck the train was a minute or two late. He caught it as usual.

XVI

The Enthusiast

Some men are born to greatness, others somehow just miss it: a few attain a kind of minor greatness of their own through a moment of sheer audacity, or perhaps a gesture of grand defiance. Among the latter I think we can safely put Mr Harold K. Wheeler whose magnificent obession, beginning with all the aspects of low comedy, may be said finally to have attained the peaks of high tragedy.

When this story begins Mr Wheeler was working – as he had worked relentlessly for some 25 years – to keep a wife and four growing greedy children. It is not important at what Mr Wheeler worked: suffice to say it brought in a rather inadequate income out of which he found it difficult to pay his way, let alone put anything aside. Yet, somehow, secretively, over all those twenty-five years, Mr Wheeler had managed to do both. During all that time he had kept clearly before him a single all-obsessive goal, the attainment of which depended primarily upon the accumulation of a certain sum of money. When Mr Wheeler's secret bank balance showed in black lettering the requisite figure he went into his bank, as calm and collected as if drawing his weekly cheque, and proceeded to draw out, in toto, the not inconsiderable sum of one thousand pounds.

Mr Wheeler knew exactly what he was going to do with his money. At a certain large motor car showroom not too far away, among dozens of bright, garish, horrid new cars, there was one car that was an exception. Unlike the new cars it was not small and compact, but vast and spacious; not tinselly and mass-produced, but heavily brassy and individually hand-made; not glittering with false promises but glowing with a mature reflection of past achievements ... In short, to Mr Wheeler's worshipful gaze, it was a car among cars, a positively mechanical Titan, a Czar among the dull proletariat. No matter that it bore the stamp of great age, was indubitably a product of the faraway nineteen-twenties, showed signs even of the sedateness of the elderly – no matter, here by George, was a *car*, a long, sleek, glowing, glistening thing of beauty from another era, to put our modern monstrosities to shame.

For two years, no less, Mr Wheeler had worshipped, or rather coveted, this car. One day the management had put it in a corner of their showroom, more as light relief than with any serious hope of a sale, and that afternoon, on the way home from work, Mr Wheeler's dreamy gaze had become fixed, once and forever, upon this sudden miraculous marvel. After that he had come to pay homage every single day, even wherever possible on rest days. With time, growing bolder, he had ventured inside the showroom for closer, even more rapturous inspection. Once he even had the temerity to inquire the price, and the figure named, though a shock, was not – by comparison to his steadily accumulating savings – an impossible one.

So when now Mr Wheeler walked boldly into the showroom and informed a rather dazed young car salesman that he had come to purchase the car of his dream and would they please have it brought round to his home – he was still able to depart with several hundreds of pounds remaining in his account. This was just as well, for Mr Wheeler's magnificent obsession was only at the beginning of its fulfilment.

First it was necessary for Mr Wheeler to have to himself the whole of the surburban garage attached to one side of his semi-detached house. This meant the cursory disposal of a variety of alien objects, including various packing cases of his wife's, his eldest son's motor cycle, his second son's scooter, and his two younger children's bicycles. Out, out they must go – out on to the front lawn for their owners to worry about.

Next, for he had taken careful measurements, it was necessary to uproot the garden gates, which were simply not wide enough for the new tenant of the garage – this Mr Wheeler did with a kind of maniacal strength of his own, leaving a trail of wreckage along his wife's favourite bed of sweetbriars. He had just finished when the car, looking even more prehistoric in the setting of a tree-lined suburban avenue, purred impressively to a stop outside. A few minutes later, under Mr Wheeler's anxious guidance, the mechanic had reversed the car neatly into the garage, departing rather surprised with a pound note tip – and Mr Wheeler was at last alone with a creature (he suddenly realised) he loved more than anything else in the world.

Mr Wheeler realised this, in fact, because of the detached, almost casual way in which he received the angry complaints and protests from his family.

'You'll just have to find somewhere else for the scooter and bikes, won't you? It's too bad, but I need the garage – now.'

Now. This was a new, wonderful, exciting word in Mr Wheeler's not very notable vocabulary. For him everything, a whole new world, began from now. At last his magnificent obsession had been obtained – and must now be magnificently observed and fulfilled.

Mr Wheeler had long since decided on his course of action. First he obtained enormous quantities of Brasso and polish and silicones, then he set to work to rub them all devoutly into the somewhat dulled-down body of his new mistress. For hour after hour he worked in his shirt-sleeves, latterly by electric light, completely ignoring requests to enter his home for meals. About two o'clock in the morning, a little weary, he took a quick nap by the sitting room fire. At seven he was out again, rubbing and polishing.

At eight o'clock his wife peered round the door, worriedly.

'You'll be late for work, won't you?'

'I'm not going to work,' said Mr Wheeler brusquely. 'Tell them I'm ill – got the flu. Go on, woman. I'm busy.'

In both his tone to his wife and his easy assumption of deceitfulness Mr Wheeler showed a remarkable and, to his wife, alarming change of character. She went back in the house shaking her head, and there followed an anxious family conflab, from which nothing definite resulted. Had they but known it, this was merely the beginning of Mr Wheeler's saga.

Two days later Mr Wheeler managed to go back to work for a day, but he was really worried all the time about checking the dynamo and the ignition wiring, he wanted to make quite sure everything was in working order before consummating his new relationship. Better get in that fellow from the garage down the road who'd showed some interest. Yes ... better really if he was there to explain things, yes.

In the morning Mr Wheeler unexpectedly had flu again, and spent the day very happily in the garage with a taciturn but interested mechanic called Fred. Mr Wheeler was able, delightedly, to indulge in such remarks as:

'They don't make them like this any more, do they?'

Simply in order to savour the full emphatic flavour of Fred's:

'Not blooming likely, they don't.'

When Mr Wheeler and the mechanic had finished with the Old Lady, as the new acquisition became christened, they had achieved quite a transformation. Colours that had faded and lain dormant suddenly spurted into flaming new life: brass glowed, chrome shone, silver-plate glittered, the vast black leather roof glistened from waxing: the interior fittings had been spruced up and looked suitably opulent and luxurious. Altogether here was a car fit for a monarch, and a monarch was precisely what Mr Wheeler felt himself to be when at last, cautiously and considerately, he went for his first jaunt with the Old Lady. A monarch of all he surveyed, sitting proud as a peacock high up in the leather-plush driving seat, nodding and smiling and waving (and indeed, somewhat vulgarly perhaps, winking) to his startled neighbours.

But of course, Mr Wheeler reflected, no decent monarch would dream of making an appearance in baggy grey flannels and an old jacket – no, it was an insult to the Old Lady. What he needed was a complete outfit of new clothes more suited to his new position – and by George, he would pull up outside the most expensive outfitters and see to the matter at once.

When Mr Wheeler emerged again he was wearing

appropriate and very expensive tweeds, a leather motoring coat and a rather gay straw hat. He looked a bit of a lad somehow – and he felt one, too. This he thought, taking possession once more of his new love, was the Life.

After this exciting expedition in which he tasted the first fruits of the exotic life, Mr Wheeler, as the saying goes, changed. It was as if some rebellious questing spirit, long incarcerated within his humble frame, had suddenly been set free and now soared at will about the open sky. His own family, to use their phrase, 'Did not know him any more'. Mr Wheeler's attendance at meals became erratic, his visits to the office increasingly infrequent, his absorption with the constant demands of the Old Lady almost total.

Money was no object. Mr Wheeler soon got through his remaining two or three hundred purchasing little trinkeries for his car – an old-fashioned brass side-lamp, new tyres to special measurements, brass number plates, tapestry curtains for the interior, a new set of cushions, a foot muff, a bell cord for calling the chauffeur's attention ... Several times, indeed, Mr Wheeler played dangerously with the idea of engaging a full-time chauffeur, as only befitting such a regal car: what stopped him was no consideration of cost but a grudging unwillingness to forfeit the sensual pleasure of driving the Old Lady up and down his local High Street.

Soon Mr Wheeler came to the end of his savings, and there was nothing for it but to make a quick and pretty ruthless appraisement of his weekly economic distribution of his wage packet.

'I'm afraid, dear,' he said absently to his aghast wife, 'you and the children will have to manage more efficiently – I can't possibly spare more than half the usual housekeeping. You see, she only does eight miles to the gallon and then there's oil and upkeep, oh and a hundred and one things.'

That of course was only a beginning. After a few weeks the housekeeping was reduced still further, finally curtailed altogether. After all, Mr Wheeler reasoned, he had two grown up sons at work, let them keep the family. His own physical needs, goodness knew, were frugal enough.

The Old Lady's, however, seemed inexhaustible. As was the way of things, with regular use there came inevitable minor – sometimes even major – breakdowns. Mr Wheeler, previously the most upright of men, became an expert sponger, at first on his bewildered sons, later on any friend or casual acquaintance who happened to come along. Five pounds or five shillings, it was all grist to his mill, a gallon of petrol at the very worst.

By now Mr Wheeler had been dismissed from his job. It wasn't, Mr Wheeler's superior explained, so much that the firm objected to his parking that extraordinary vehicle outside all day causing crowds of sight-seers to accumulate; it wasn't just that Mr Wheeler's attendance chart had fallen catastrophically, even below the fifty-five mark; it wasn't *just* even that Mr Wheeler appeared to spend a large part of his time doodling drawings of cars on scraps of paper – no, it was simply the *accumulation* of all these irritations.

Prodded by his insatiable need for petrol money Mr Wheeler now went on the dole, later on to National Assistance, both procedures which would have been unimaginable to the old Mr Wheeler. To the new, magnificently obsessed Mr Wheeler they were mere procedures, means to an end. Needless to say he found it impossible to spare any of the money for his wife and family, who so far had managed to struggle on precariously on the small income of the two boys. Now, seeing at last that Mr Wheeler was beyond redemption, his wife took her children with her and went to stay with some kindly relatives.

Mr Wheeler was quite glad to be rid of such irritating worries. Now that he had the house to himself he felt able to concentrate more completely on his own problems. Soon the rooms became filled up with copies of motoring magazines, with expensive books on motoring, and with a variety of weird and wonderful spare parts for the car, most of them specially machined at great cost by high class engineering firms. Soon there was something else to fill up the space: bills, rows and humps and hillocks and veritable mountains of bills – for gradually Mr Wheeler was losing his financial battle.

But somehow he managed to keep everyone and everything

at bay until the day of his great triumph, the day of days when proudly he drove the Old Lady in that famed annual event, the Old Crocks Race to Brighton. If you happened to be there at all you may well have seen Mr Harold K. Wheeler in his greatest hour, seated spruce and sartorially perfect high up at the driving wheel of that elegant and most impressive motor car: the brass glowing, the bodywork shining, the whole ensemble a veritable work of art.

As he proudly drove the Old Lady down the Brighton road on that memorable day I think we may truly say that the magnificent obsession of Mr Wheeler found its magnificent fulfilment. Better, don't you think, to take our leave of him there than to follow him into the depressing anti-climactic world of debts and writs, bailiffs and sheriffs, closures and perhaps ultimate bankruptcy – even, who knows, the loss of the beloved one and a resigned return to that old humdrum life. No, no – let us not dwell on the gloomier aspect of things. Let us do homage instead to one of those rare beings who, in a world of conformity, brought a magnificent obsession to a magnificent reality.

Salute, Mr Harold K. Wheeler!

XVII

A Ring for Remembrance

When I was a boy I used to spend the summer holidays at Llantyllan on the sea-washed tip of the North Wales coast. My parents went there each year because we could stay with my Aunt Lil, who had a small boarding house on the promenade – and really, what more could you ask for than the sea and the sand at your doorstep, the shimmering vista of Anglesey on the horizon?

From morning to night we would spend our time on the golden sands, sometimes venturing for a change along the grey cobbled road that led to the top of Bryn Glas. Yes, they were happy, magical days. It was at Llantyllan that I captured something secret and wonderful about the meaning of life, the marvellous experience of living in the golden moment.

And it was at Llantyllan that I met Dwyffryd.

She was seventeen then, brown as a berry from the summer sun, her black hair falling long and loose down her back. When she went bathing or to church she would wear it coiled up on the back of her head. But when she came walking along the Cob or when we ran hand in hand across the mountainside she let it stream out, the winds plucking at the tresses and wafting them out like waves.

We were always laughing and teasing each other, but behind it all lay something else. For hadn't we walked together along the Cob so many evenings hand in hand, content just to be together in a curious, silent sort of communion? Hadn't we climbed the boulder-strewn sides of Bryn Glas to the grassy plateau at the top, and then sat staring out across the white-crested waves of the Irish sea towards fantasy images of white horsemen clouds riding the horizon? And hadn't we, that very afternoon, turned suddenly towards one another, as if bidden by some unseen force to do so, and embraced silently but finally?

We were happy that idyllic summer, Dwyffryd and I. We knew when we sat on the pebbles at night and tossed small round stones gently into the swirling waters that the August moon, the stars and the night itself were for us alone.

One night I twined strands of green grass into a ring and, when I slipped it gently on to Dwyffryd's finger, we felt solemn, as if we were in church.

' 'Till death do us part, darling,' I whispered.

And she whispered back, ' 'Till death do us part … '

But it wasn't anything so romantic as death that parted us soon after. It was the end of the holiday and, for me, a return to London: but worse, the discovery that Dwyffryd's parents were taking her abroad on a long visit to Australia, where she had some relatives. That meant that when the next summer holidays came round …

'I shan't come,' I said grimly. 'I couldn't bear to be here without you.'

I didn't, either. Not the next year, nor the one after that. But before she went away Dwyffryd had promised me that on the first day of September in three years time, at eight o'clock in the evening, come what may we would meet once more at our secret place on top of Bryn Glas. And nothing would stop me from fulfilling that pact.

I caught the night train from London and spent the day at Caernarvon, at last taking the chocolate coloured bus over to Llantyllan.

I had often imagined the moment when I was on top of Bryn Glas again … how I would lean over the boulder at the top of the track and see the wisp of Dwyffryd's skirt as she came round the bend … how I would leap down the path to hold her once again in my arms … I had not imagined much beyond that, but I had experienced that supreme moment again and again.

But now reality was different. Though I stared until my eyes

ached I could see no wisp of colour, no stir of human life –
only the old familiar pattern, the yellow gorse bushes and the
empty, winding track.

I waited and waited, until it was nearly dusk, and then I went
down into the village. But nobody there could help me,
nobody knew when Dwyffryd might return. She had been away
a long time. In the end I caught the last bus to Caernarvon and
then the night express back to London, and I tried to forget.

It took me a long time. Years, in fact. The years in which we
grow up, in which we change, in which we work and travel and
inevitably form new ties – in which, indeed, we marry and have
families.

Last year, I don't quite know why, we decided to spend our
summer holiday touring Wales … One night we camped in the
flat fields below Llantyllan.

I don't know whether it was planned that way, or not – who
knows these things? But my wife felt tired and wanted to go to
bed early, so I said casually:

'I used to know these parts. I think I'll take a stroll up the
mountain, just for old times' sake.'

I suppose I shouldn't have gone. Even as I took the winding
track I was remembering those other time when I ran up arm
in arm with the girl on whose finger I had, so confidently,
slipped my grass ring.

It was still quite light when I reached the top and sat on the
great flat stone that had been our meeting place. I lay back on
the stone, dreaming, while the red orange ball of the sun sank
behind Anglesey.

At last, with a sigh, I got up to go. And it was then that my
foot dislodged the slate, and I remembered our secret hiding
place, where we used to leave messages. On the last occasion I
had searched there in vain … but NOW I found there was
something, a small parcel.

I pulled it out nervously, unravelling that crumpled paper,
damp from years of lying in the crevice. I opened out the
contents – and there, in the evening light, lay a slip of paper –
and my old grass ring.

I can remember staring at the ring as if I would never look

anywhere else again: and then turning at last to the scrap of paper on which, perhaps twenty years ago now, Dwyffryd had sadly written: *My darling, I came back – but the boat was delayed and I was two days late. I love you, so come for me. If not, this ring will be in remembrance. Your loving Dwyffryd.*

Underneath was the address where she must have stayed – and waited.

I went to the edge of the plateau. The sun had now almost set and a kind of sad, fading light surrounded Anglesey – shrouding the sea, the whole of the world that had once been lit by my youthful dreams.

'Oh, Dwyffryd!' I cried out. 'Oh, Dwyffryd, my love!'

And then, before the tears of twenty years could flood back from the past to engulf the precious present, I threw away that dead grass ring and ran all the way down that winding mountain track – down to the neat white canopy of the children's tent, the familiar shape of the car in which my wife lay sleeping peacefully. Quietly, so as not to disturb her, I crept into bed and lay still: and, moving casually in her sleep, my wife burrowed her head into my shoulder.

In the morning, early, I drove away, taking with me the world that is – and leaving to the haunting winds of Bryn Glas the world that might have been.

XVIII

The Factory

The factory is quite unostentatious, a neat pattern of grey-green strips, blending so smoothly into the contours of the landscape that only at close quarters is it possible to distinguish between green grassland and camouflaged tarmac roofing. For this reason hardly anyone in the outside world is aware of the factory's existence, a condition of inestimable advantage to the Management, who are thus able to devote undistracted attention to their revolutionary task of creating an entirely new order of society. The exact nature of this order is difficult to define in a few words, but the essential basis is Full Productivity. It is quite obvious, as the Management point out, that a society of fully employed workers must be a successful society. Now that the semblance of such a society is indeed taking shape this may be an appropriate moment to consider, in a spirit of due reverence and admiration, something of the achievement of its sponsors.

Designed on the maxim that is indeed the working principle of the Management's whole policy – namely, that Full Efficiency is the essential pre-requisite of Full Productivity – the factory is a masterpiece of planning and organisation, covering as it does an area of many square miles. The main buildings are all of the same single-storey design, with walls and roofs made of extra-strengthened steel and re-inforced concrete. Special pipe lines convey all forms of smoke, dust and dirt to a central smoke-abatement and odour-disposal plant. For security and other reasons there are no windows, but an intricate combination of scientific air-conditioning and fluorescent tube-lighting not only conveys the effect of external conditions but actually produces a stimulative effect estimated to be considerably more potent than ordinary air and sunlight. Everything is ultra-clean, ultra-bright, ultra-efficient and ultra-fresh, from the smallest cog of machinery (which is oiled and lubricated every twenty-four hours by automatic mechanism) to the worker himself (who is also automatically washed and antiseptised every twelve hours). Similar conditions prevail at the series of workers' hostels which are set in neat rows around the outer edges of the factory, and reached by means of floodlit covered-in corridors. It is unfortunately equally impracticable for the hostels to have real windows, but the Management have spared no expense to ensure that every block, indeed, every room, is fully equipped with its own individually-controlled heat, light and air supply. Both the central and outer buildings are built to the most modern designs and supplied with every possible labour-saving, time-saving and thought-saving device. Undoubtedly – with the possible exception of real sunlight and a view of real countryside (both of which are quite adequately replaced by violet-ray lamps and colourful interior landscape pictures) – it is true to say that the factory is completely self-contained.

The most striking thing to a visitor – that is, of course, if visitors were allowed – would no doubt be the sense of beautiful rhythm with which the factory operates. This is achieved in a number of ways, not least being the fact that work is carried on continuously in six-hourly shifts. Another important arrangement is one by which each worker is allocated to a single movement in a particular piece of work. This is applied on a most detailed scale, and to such lengths that one worker will pour liquid into a container, another will insert a cork in the container and a third will pick up the container and turn it upside down to see if it is airtight – three actions which could have been done by one worker, possibly in the same amount of time, but at a lower rate of thoroughness. (At one time, of course, such work would in any case have been done by machinery, but re-adjustments are often necessary under the Management's policy – if they seem a little strange now they will be quite clearly understood later on.) The great advantage of this system is that workers, having only a single action to perform and knowing that it is likely to be their only one throughout a lifetime, are able to bring to it the most complete powers of concentration. As a further aid, the Management have so arranged production that each process of work is carried out in a separate building, the workers of which are not allowed to visit other buildings, nor to discuss their tasks with workers outside. An obvious reason for this is the fact that, if workers were to attempt to grasp the complex ramifications of the entire factory they would become so bewildered that their own production would be retarded. It is an important part of the Management's widespread internal propaganda to draw attention to this danger by means of such striking headlines as WHAT DO YOU KNOW ABOUT XYLENOL-FORALDEHYDE? or WHAT IS A BESSEMER FOR? Underneath these headings are captions pointing out frankly to the worker that no doubt he does not know the answer to such questions – which only goes to prove that his best way of getting on in the world is to concentrate upon the one piece of work in which he specialises. From there posters usually pass smoothly into the fundamental philosophy so patiently expounded by the Management: that the basis of life is Full Productivity, that only a Fully Efficient worker can give Full Productivity, hence the duty of each worker to render himself efficient according to the standards of the factory. A reminder is given of the extremely careful attention given by the Management to the comfort and entertainment of the worker while at work – examples of this are listed, such as (1) continuous broadcasts of gramophone records, titles of which workers are allowed to choose for themselves, (2) provision of air-cushioned seats and a variety of useful materials for cleaning off dirt, chemicals, poisonous dyes, etc., as well as individual first-aid boxes for immediate on-the-spot use, (3) frequent free issues of vitamin pills, calorie capsules and deficiency-replacement drinks, (4) regular disinfection of rooms and workshops by a wide variety of patent and highly-advertised chemical insecticides, (5) helpful advisory visits of time-study technicians who explain methods by which workers can increase their rate of work by 100, 200, sometimes even 300 per cent., (6) offers of valuable prizes of savings certificates and free insurance premiums for workers who surpass their fellows in output. Finally there is an impressive outline of even wider facilities provided by the Management to enable workers to keep themselves fit and productive in off-duty hours.

Before going on to consider these facilities a word might not be out of place about the workers themselves. There are many thousands of them and they are of all ages, sizes and shapes, and of both sexes. Such facts are considered generally irrelevant, however, and in order to prevent their intrusion upon the ordered procedure, every worker is issued with a pair of blue overalls, a blue beret and a pair of blue-tinted glasses (found to be necessary to counteract certain injurious effects of the lighting). In this way an impression of pleasant uniformity and subdued standardisation is achieved. In addition, as a natural development of the idea, every worker possesses a number which is sewn in white tape on his or her back. In order to avoid unnecessary confusion between names off-duty and numbers on-duty, numbers were some time ago appointed by order, to be the sole means of reference at all time. This presented certain difficulties at first, especially in connection with marriages, births and social events, but the Department of Statistics was able to provide many ingenious solutions. In the very early days a limited number of workers were recruited from outside but the day is fast approaching when all such recruitment will cease. Already several thousands of boys and girls, children of factory workers who have been born and bred on the premises, are nearing the time when they will be due to leave the factory school and fill various vacancies arising from deaths by accidents, industrial diseases, etc. Henceforward, by means of propoganda schemes to encourage a higher birth-rate, the stoppage of all supplies of birth control requisites, and the offer of various monetary enticements and grants, the Management have every hope that more than sufficient new labour replacements will be available from within the factory. Not the least of the attractions of such a scheme, and one that is prominently featured in the Management's advertisements, is the fact that parents are saved all worry as to their children's future – knowing, too, that at the end of education there awaits a guaranteed job. It is obviously a very small obligation that parents should in return provide their signatures to documents testifying that on no account will they or their children seek employment elsewhere. In the first place, practically nothing is known about opportunities for employment outside the factory. In the second place, the known is always preferable to the unknown, and as every worker ultimately reasons, he or she is hardly likely to find employment where eighteen hours of leisure time is available. In the third place, although this fact is kept discreetly in the background and only made clear in extreme cases the factory is completely isolated from external communication with the exception of a heavily guarded entrance and an equally heavily guarded exit. Coincident with their policy of reducing and finally abolishing intake of labour it is only natural that the Management should have instituted a restriction – and finally a ban – on leaving the factory.

Next to the efficient maintenance of the factory machinery, the Management's first concern is for the health and happiness of their workers. Well might they have argued that their duties in this matter were confined to the six-hourly periods spent at work, but far from doing this they have nobly undertaken complete responsibility for attending to the welfare of their workers. It is very much to their credit that when, in the earliest days, certain well meaning workers suggested that they could themselves organise their own leisure time, the Management refused to shirk their responsibilities. Moreover they tackled the matter with the same swift efficiency as has been so consistently displayed in the field of factory production. Today there is certainly not a single digit, or rather worker, who can pretend that he or she has a moment of wasted time to spare, apart from the Six Hours Sleep (Maximum) prescribed by the

Factory Medical Officer, the two Ten Minute Relaxation Periods prescribed by the Factory Psychologist, or perhaps the twenty-four One Minute Mass Meditations organised, at the stroke of each hour, upon the order of the Spiritual Development Officer. Every day there is a six-hourly programme of sports, entertainment, meetings, social events and so on, the programme being repeated for the benefit of each shift, so that there shall be no resentment among workers that perhaps members of another shift are securing some invidious advantage. As far as possible the competitive spirit is encouraged – i.e., there are football leagues composed of teams representing different buildings in the factory – as the sentimental attraction of this tends to provide yet one more incentive for a worker to remain where he is. In the case of meetings, dramatics, etc., in order to save unnecessary brain fatigue on the part of workers, the Management themselves undertake the very arduous task of selecting subjects. The efficiency of this system is recognised by all, although there have been occasions when it had diffidently been suggested that, by way of a change, workers should choose their own subjects. To these infrequent requests the Management are only too ready to agree and at once hold a ballot vote, each worker writing down on a piece of paper his or her suggestion. The papers are then collected into a container and handed to two tellers, usually the Works Manager and the Chairman of the Board, who retire into the former's office and very ably make the count. When the results are announced no one can fail to be impressed at the striking way in which the workers' own choice invariably falls into identical line with the type of suggestions usually put forward by the Management.

It is one of the Management's proudest boasts that there exists among the workers of the factory a most generous allowance of freedom of speech. Indeed, in order to encourage this the Management have made it a factory rule that 'at very frequent intervals' – (that is the exact phrase) – 'open meetings shall be held for the free expression and discussion of politics, social reform and reconstruction.' In view of this special facility, and so as not to cause confusion or diffusion of interests, the Management have also most wisely added a further rule to the effect that no public meetings or discussions attended by more than two people may be held within the factory precincts, other than on the occasions specified. At the official open meetings some most interesting speeches are given by the Chairman, the Works Manager, the Production Manager, the Welfare Manager, the Education Officer, the Medical Officer, the Transport Manager, and others Afterwards there is a half-hour Question Time, during which members of the audience are invited to express their viewpoints. These are listened to with great care, and the names of the speakers noted, as it is a firm maxim of the Management always to be on the look-out for workers who show signs of initiative and self-confidence. Almost inevitably, within a short time, every one of these speakers receives notification that he or she has been promoted, and is invited to report, with family if there is one, to the Central Transference Department, for posting to higher office. Thenceforth, as it is a rule of the factory that communication between departments is forbidden, no further word is ever heard from the promotee. However, inquirers have only to apply to the Welfare Manager to receive a very encouraging report upon their friend's progress. In this way former friends can feel a continued sense of contact even though the worker could be said, in a way, to have entirely disappeared.

Workers are allowed similar freedom of religious worship, and the Management in their benevolence have provided buildings to suit every conceivable type of religious denomination – and moreover, have provided their own personal staff of ministers, one to each place of worship. The skill with which these holy men explain, text by text from Biblical and other religious sources, exactly how the Management's policy is practically identical with that of Jesus Christ, is something which has to be seen to be fully appreciated. Apart from religion and the dramas, the subject of the workers' minds is constantly under review and a very thorough educational service is provided. This is divided into two sections – education for adults and education for children.

In the case of children it is possible to make a fresh start entirely untrammelled by influences of old-fashioned systems of education, and schedules of classes are drawn up which are designed to introduce the child at once to the really practical and necessary matters with which he will be primarily concerned in adult life – that is, the basic rudiments of the particular piece of work he will take up on joining the factory. The simplicity of this system, and its advantages for the child, are obvious, for he or she is enabled to take up work in life fully equipped and trained. Under the old system the child would have had a confused and unnecessary knowledge of all manner of subjects, such as geography, history, French, Latin, economics, arithmetic, etc. – but little or no knowledge of the far more fundamental subject of, for instance, the most efficient human usage of the moving conveyor belt. Indeed, under the factory's educational system it has been found possible, thanks to an increasing ability to dispense with a very wide list of escapist subjects, to so train children that they are able to take up employment sometimes at the ages of 12 or even 10. They are then extremely favourably placed for earning one of the various Management Badges of Honour (silver stars embossed with an etching of a factory chimney) which are awarded to all workers whose period of service reaches 60 years. While at school, apart from their main training, the children are given courses in physical drill and other sports, so that their fitness will be of the high standard necessary to enable them to withstand the various and sometimes unfortunately rather overstraining conditions of work within the factory. They are also encouraged to take an interest in literature, and to learn by heart large sections of the many attractive pamphlets and books issued by the Factory Publications Department, as well as to read carefully through each day's issue of the *Factory Daily News*. Lest it be thought, however, that the literature classes are at all narrow in approach, it should be mentioned that a regular feature of every class syllabus is the learning by heart of a book of 300 *Poems in Praise of Increased Production*, written by Soviet Russian proletarian poets, and dedicated to leading Stahkanovites – a book which the Management considered themselves most fortunate in coming across as it was found that workers at once accepted the entire gospel as soon as the country of its origin was mentioned. Indeed the same book is always a prominent feature of the numerous production drives the Management consider it wise to sponsor whenever the slightest suspicion of what might remotely be called discontent can be detected. It also forms an important item in the adult education scheme which, as mentioned, differs somewhat from the youth education, owing to the fact that here the teachers have sometimes to deal with people who have been unfortunate enough to have passed in their youth through all the misdirected phases of a conventional education system. The longer their sojourn in the factory, the more readily, or rather the less unwillingly, do the workers agree to the wisdom of the new methods. In the case of the very obstreperous, these misguided people are given the benefit of a course of special treatment at the Factory's Psychiatry Centre – a rather specialised establishment that is, like the Factory hospital, established in an isolated and somewhat separated part of the factory premises. Such treatment may require a considerable passage of time and, such is the public memory, before long everyone has completely forgotten about the absent patient – so that no one is every really interested to know why he or she never returns. In the meantime, adult education or re-education proceeds with increasing smoothness; already the Management can congratulate themselves that they are reaching nearer and nearer to their ideal of finding a common denominator (not necessarily the lowest) at which the minds of the children and the minds of the adults can be said to find a level.

The problem of health is another important consideration of the factory Management and they operate a most comprehensive Health Service, available from birth to death. This being, obviously, a specialised department, requiring specialised knowledge, the Management have trained their own Medical Department, to whom complete authority is given. This in turn, has provided the Medical Department with unequalled opportunities for research work, such as into the effect upon productive output of the application of various chemical stimulants, glandular treatments, and so on. Nor can the charge of restrictive orthodoxy be levelled, for, in the cause of the advancement of medical science, the Medical Officer himself has supervised a number of interesting experiments in hypnotism, in process of which it was found possible to empty a worker's mind of all thoughts except the one expressed in the phrase: "I must turn the screw! I must turn the screw!" – and equally to concentrate his entire physical powers on to this single task. The results, in terms of increased production, were astounding. The Works Manager himself was heard to point out that only if the process could be carried a bit further human workers would soon be able to equalise the performance of machines. In reply the Medical Officer pointed out, thoughtfully but not without optimism, that he was already working on a process for partial paralysis of the brain which might have just the desired effect ... But of course, these experiments are merely one of the Department's activities. There is, for example, a most intricate system of inoculation, under which a worker can be inoculated every day of the year against a different disease. The following year he then takes a precautionary treatment, under which he is inoculated to protect him against possible after-effects of the original inoculations. The number of deaths from original inocul- ations have in this way been considerably reduced and, although statistics have yet to be collected as to rate of deaths in relation to anti-inoculation, there is no reason to suppose that here again, medical ingenuity will not find a solution. There is no need, and no space, to go here into the details of the many brilliant surgical operations performed by the factory doctors – enough to mention that it is their proud claim now that, except for actual death, they can patch up any worker, no matter how badly injured or mangled he might be as the result of one of the unfortunate accidents that occur during the course of a day. Furthermore, thanks to the system of standardised blue overalls, it is very frequently possible for workers to avoid feeling uncomfortable about wooden legs, wooden arms and other disabilities – and also, incidentally to avoid offending the peace of mind of fellow workers.

There are a very large number of other matters which it would be most interesting to discuss here were it not for space – feeding, clothing, wages and so on – but which can be summarised by mentioning that in nearly every case the fortunate worker is entirely absolved from having to waste time, energy and brain-power on needless worrying. Instead of having to spend hours wondering whether he can afford to buy this or that, whether he should eat this or that, whether he should wear this or that suit, the worker finds that the decisions are taken for him by the Management. Each week he is issued with a number of credit notes which entitle him and his family to a given number of articles – i.e. one steak, one pound of butter, so many pounds of vegetables, so many pints of milk, one pair of socks (or pants, as the case may be), two library books, three packets of cigarettes, one chair, one set of dominoes, etc. (In the case of a woman worker the articles vary accordingly). The worker concerned then only has to present the notes at a Regional Supply Depot and he will at once be supplied with the articles listed. Sometimes, of course, a worker might not actually consider himself in need of a wooden chair, or a set of dominoes, but he is reminded that sooner or later the need *will* arise. Similarly, should he express a desire to have some article not on the list – perhaps a blanket or a cake – his desire is regretfully turned down with the reminder that in due course he will undoubtedly receive credit notes for such articles. What with the issue of these notes and with free admission to all organised entertainment, the worker has no need for actual money: accordingly he is not paid wages in cash. However, extremely large credit balances are entered in the worker's savings account and placed in reserve for use, should he wish, in old age. The Management have always found that the anticipation of receiving a large sum of saved money, plus the knowledge that free accommodation and excellent board is provided in the luxurious Old Age Pensioners Home, has proved a definite incentive to higher output on the part of workers approaching retirement age. It remains a matter for concern that every single worker, upon reaching retirement age and entering into the restful and leisured life of the Pensioners Home, quickly becomes ill and dies, even though he or she might never have had a day's illness before. The clear opinion of the Medical Officer is that this relapse is due to the fact that workers – having become adapted over a period of about sixty years to passing through a series of identical physical movements, perhaps several thousand times a day – find themselves entirely without the strength to re-adapt themselves to a routine of doing nothing at all, beyond sitting in an armchair or walking round a rose garden. It is therefore his somewhat unanswerable diagnosis that if a worker, on reaching retirement age, wishes to live in continued good health, the only possible method is for him to carry on with his work. The Management have accepted the logic of this; but since the productive capacity of such workers would become consistently lower and lower, they have decided that in the circumstances the present system might as well be carried on.

This brief and inadequate survey may give some idea of the intricate working of the highly organised society of which the factory is the home, and must arouse considerable envy in the minds of millions of unfortunate people still enduring the iniquities and corruptions of less purposeful regimes. At the same time it is necessary, in conclusion, to touch on one further issue since this, perhaps more than anything, demonstrates the inherent genius of the factory Management. As a matter of historical interest, the factory came into existence during a time of war, when there was a steady demand for the products of war. During the period of the war the factory flourished and expanded, employing a steadily increasing number of well paid workers and – as the Management must even then have realised – presenting an illuminating example of the Fully Productive Society. The end of the war came suddenly, and raised grave issues. Pending another war, what could the factory produce that would find the same ready outlet in a peacetime and partially ruined world? For a time it was found possible to carry on reduced production of small arms for supplying to various guerrilla

armies and to certain South American States, but even these
orders dwindled and dwindled. Just when the situation seemed
at its worst, the Management hit on the remarkable idea of
Production for Re-Purchase – a system which would at least
enable the factory and its machines to be kept in production.
At once an ambitious programme was launched for the
production of a wide variety of munitions, small arms, gas
bombs, etc. These were then sold to the workers, who paid for
them out of credit notes issued by the Management's private
printing press. The workers of course had no immediate use
for such materials, but facilities were provided for storing them
away, as there was always the possibility that some day war
would return and they would then prove extremely useful.
Meantime, since the factory was one of the few in the country
able to announce a steady rise of productive output, despite all
external slumps, it rapidly attracted more and more financial
backing from investors. With the vast funds thus accumulated,
and before it became necessary to pay out any dividends, the
Management, through judicious manipulation of stocks and
shares, were able themselves to make financial profits large
enough to meet the factory's production costs for at least 1000
years ahead (not to mention a handsome repayment of
investors). The only real difficulty remaining was how to
accommodate the vast stocks of materials that were accumulating? This was solved by a final stroke of genius, the S.P.U-P.
R-P. – or, the System of Production for Un-Production and
Re-Production. Under this, to cut a long story short, raw
materials entering the factory at one end pass through a series
of manufacturing processes which result in their emerging as
finished products just as they reach a series of buildings in the
middle of the factory. Passing through the remaining half of
the factory the finished products are, by means of similar
processes, re-converted back into the original raw materials.
Finally, these raw materials are transported from the exit to the
entrance of the factory, where they are entered as before, and
the process repeated. In order to avoid unnecessary
bewilderment, the workers are not actually informed of the
final destination of the products they work upon, but it is quite

obvious to them that they are doing creative and purposeful work.

It would be difficult to over-estimate the achievements of the Management, to over-emphasise the brilliance of their administration, to over-praise their painstaking attention to every little detail. And yet, the question might be posed, perhaps even they, immersed in the immediate demands of their task, have over-looked one important item: is it not likely that as the years pass they will be unkindly removed from this life, even as befalls us all? But of course, this is quite inevitable and the Management have made the most careful preparations for dealing with such a development – for it would be nothing short of disastrous, in their honest view, if their policy should be interrupted just when it is perhaps becoming an example to the whole world. Consequently some twenty years ago the Management selected a group of twelve children of the age of two years, males predominating. Since then these twelve have been brought up in strict seclusion from their fellows and educated, by the most rigorous of processes, for the express purpose of taking their places on the board of the Management. Starting from a period when their thinking and talking powers were completely malleable the Management have been able to create, in these twelve fortunate individuals, a unified group of executives and technicians whose inheritance will be the glorious one of expanding the policy of Full Productivity, now firmly established at its original home, to embrace the entire world. One immediate advantage of this development will be access to a supply of human labour sufficiently large to replace machinery – a development long sought by the Management who are confident that the substitution of *elastic* human power for *inelastic* and geometrically limited machine power will offer scope (via psychological, medical, auto-reflex, hypnotic and various other scientific treatments) for the attainment of productivity on a scale at present beyond the imagination.

But that is perhaps thinking a little too far ahead. In the meantime it must be our consolation that in a world of somersaulting values and unpredictable uncertainties, of hazards and dangers beyond the capacities of all but the most foolhardy adventures, there remains the factory – symbol of safety, neatness and well-ordered discipline.

Who's for the next shift?

XIX

At the Station

The man in the anonymous grey suit had planned everything, down to the last minute detail.

He knew exactly what time the special train would arrive at the city station, the number of the platform where it would pull in, how many minutes would be spent in receiving the new ambassador before the procession moved off to the waiting cars, the order in which those cars would make their appearance, even the last conventional courtesies that must be exchanged before the ambassador bent forward to enter the waiting car ... He knew all these things because it was his job to know. He was a trained assassin, a professional killer.

And now he had been instructed to dispose of the ambassador once and for all. There must be no mistake, no slip up. The lethal weapon to accomplish his purpose lay flat and snug, and curiously cold, in his hip pocket. It had been there, guarded as preciously as any diamond, ever since he set out on his perilous journey, a long time ago.

He had chosen his position with great care, near to the western exit of the station. Once he had fired the shots there would certainly be immediate confusion and chaos ... in those vital moments he would dart round the corner, spring along the street and jump into a large delivery van that he knew was parked there every day at this time.

He knew the van would be there because he had been checking, and checking, and counter checking. Every day, he had found, this particular van drove up and unloaded and then filled up again with a pile of empty packing cases. And – this was the significant point – every day the driver went off for a cup of tea just at the time the ambassador's train was due to arrive. During those moments he would climb up into the back of the lorry and quickly hide away under one of the empty boxes ... nobody would know, nobody would be interested at such a moment in an anonymous delivery van trundling away ... he would lie there as quiet as a mouse and be carried away to safety when the driver came back and drove away.

When he finally arrived at the station there were already crowds of curious spectators waiting. They were a mixed bunch. There was one group of demonstrators carrying a huge banner of welcome for the visitor – another group, smaller, but more vocal, made no secret of their distaste. Well, everyone as they felt, he thought with a somewhat sardonic smile.

The police were there, of course, in fairly large numbers, yet trying to keep what was usually called a low profile. You could see them sizing up the groups of demonstrators, trying to assess any possible dangers. He supposed, too, that some of them would be on the look out for other dangers – some like himself, a lone wolf. They knew that their official visitor was not exactly universally popular.

After watching discreetly for a while he decided he was pleased with the way things were working out. The constant squabbling and catcalls that took place between the two groups of demonstrators kept the attentions of the police engaged, so that they really seemed to have little time for anything else. Besides, many of them were obviously young, new recruits, understandably a little jumpy.

When the train was finally signalled there was a sudden upsurge of movement, in which he allowed himself to be carried along until he found himself brought up against an iron pillar and leaned on it. He was in a good position, not more than twelve yards or so from the carpeted space which the police were deliberately keeping clear in readiness for the ceremony of welcome. He could not have chosen a better spot if he had booked a space beforehand.

As he watched, his hand already inside his pocket, fingering at the silencer, he noticed around him the various dignitaries gathering, members of the local council, no doubt the local MP, perhaps one or two cabinet ministers – yes, there was the Foreign Secretary, he recognised him from the photographs. And a mayor, complete with old-fashioned flowing robes and gold chain and curious peaked hat.

Suddenly there was a chatter of excitement as a rumble of sound heralded the long diesel train's impending arrival. At the far end of the station the gleaming snout appeared, and came gliding along ... with much hissing and snorting the train edged its way up towards the buffers and at last came to a shuddering halt.

As if at a given signal the crowd closed up, surging forward close against the tubular barriers, and the man shuffled along with them. There was a flurry of movement ahead, and the police linked arms and began to press people back, holding a line of defence.

There was a pause, and then suddenly one of the carriage doors opened. From somewhere came the beginnings of some ragged cheers. Here and there television cameramen began whirring their cameras and newspaper photographers raised their quick firing cameras and clicked away, flash bulbs popping. It was a scene that must have been enacted on this particular platform a hundred time before – for a variety of celebrities, from reigning monarchs to pop stars, from Arabian Sheiks to Western diplomats ... Well, this time the welcome was to be a different one.

Abruptly, at the doorway of the coach, appeared a smiling figure, familiar from innumerable newspaper photographs and television interviews. With professional ease and charm, as if by magic, there appeared a smile, a bow, a languid wave of the hand to acknowledge with equal affability both the cheers and the boos.

Watching, tensed, he saw the ambassador step forward onto the raised platform. A few words into the microphone – and then at last the scheduled moment. There was a pause, the ambassador stood just a little apart from his companions, waiting for the inevitable car to whisk him off on his long planned journey. It was like some immense and eternal moment in time. Now – now, now – *now*!

Swiftly he raised the pistol and fired three times. Almost at the same time he turned and hurled himself towards the exit.

As he raced round the corner he heard the sudden rising of excited voices, one or two screams. As he had calculated, the shots had had a stunning effect on everyone for a few seconds. And now, as suddenly the police jumped into action, the very density of the crowds around proved an impediment.

Looking round he saw the familiar lorry ahead of him ... He sprinted up the incline towards it. There was nobody around, he was in luck's way. With a quick flexing of his muscles he heaved himself over the back and inside. In the interior gloom he saw packing cases everywhere – *empty* packing cases.

Careful to make no noise he lifted one of the cases up in a corner of the lorry and sank down into the oblivion underneath, replacing its top cover noiselessly. Now ... he must wait.

After a while he heard the footsteps of the driver returning. He seemed not to have noticed the distant commotion, or if he did no doubt attributed it simply to the scheduled visitation. From inside the lorry the man heard the sound of the driver climbing up into the cab.

Just a few moments more and the lorry would move out and away from the station, taking him to safety.

In the distance there were cries. Would the lorry driver hear them, pause, become curious? No, he was starting the engine. It purred into action and with a jerk the lorry moved forward, quickly beginning to gather speed.

Suddenly in the rear a peremptory demand rang out, an angry and official sounding order. Abruptly the lorry driver applied his brakes and decelerated. Outside it was easy to envisage the arrival of a breathless policeman, to imagine the conversation – had there been any signs of a man running away?

Never mind, the man told himself. In a few words the lorry driver would explain that he had seen no one, the policeman would nod the all-clear, and the lorry would be off again on its unwitting escape route ...

And then it began.

The man felt a faint, irritating tickle at the back of his throat. At first it was something he hardly noticed. Then, in some ominous sort of way, it seemed to spread, to travel across the membrane like a small yet deadly tongue of fire blazing across some open stretch of tinder-dry moorland.

And now – yes now he *was* conscious of the irritation. Cooped up under the box, unable to move, he felt the back of his throat suddenly sore and twitching ... and worse, too, there was a sudden strange feeling at the back of his nostrils.

His eyes filled with sudden tears as he caught at his breath, one urgent hand clutching at his nose, trying not to swallow, trying not to breathe ... No, he mustn't – he mustn't, he simply mustn't ... He wouldn't, he dared not!

The fire burned up, the irritation rose to a sort of frenzy, while the tears streamed down his cheeks. Violently, desperately, he struggled, until he became red in the face with the effort. In anguish he turned his face from side to side, pressing his fingers against his temple, trying to distract attention from the awful festering certainty ... and then, half smothered, and at last suddenly totally released, the sound burst forth.

'Aaaa – tttt – issssssshoooooooooooo!'

'Aaaa – tttt – issssssshhoooooo!'

Again and again and again.

'Aaaa – ttt – issssshoooooo!'

'Aaaa – tttt – issssshooooo!'

It seemed to the crouching man that the sound was like the crashing of cymbals, many times in succession. It echoed and re-echoed in the confined space of the packing box until he could well imagine that the box itself was beginning to sway and rock from the violence of the movement and the disturbance.

'Aaaaa – tttt – issssssshoooo!'

Again and again and again he sneezed ... on and on and on it went, as if he would never be able to stop again, never in his life.

He was still crouched there sneezing helplessly when the two policemen came round to the back of the lorry, kicking away a small empty box marked PEPPER – and proceeded to lift the top of the large case and expose the man they had hardly expected to catch, gun still warm in his pocket.

XX

Just a Song at Twilight

The trouble with that piano was that we never knew where to put it. It was so heavy, you didn't feel like moving it about much, anyway.

But sometimes one of us revolted. I remember the time my sister, Amy, called in three strapping fellows from her office to move it out of her cramped little bedroom. You could hardly blame her, really.

When we came home that evening, there the piano was, in the hall. For several weeks afterwards, to get in and out of the house, we had to hold our breath and squeeze by the piano, or, like my kid brother, Johnny, crawl along the floor under the keyboard.

Mother didn't seem to mind. She used the back door mostly anyway, as it led straight into the kitchen. But if you said anything to her, she just muttered: 'Your father … '

And if we took the complaint to Father, he just shook his head knowingly and said: 'Your mother … '

Naturally, we knew that Mother and Father were very much attracted to the old piano. It had been a wedding present from the couple who had owned the café, and every night someone would play their favourite tunes.

The place had closed down just before Mother and Father were married, and the owners, who knew my parents so well by this time, had given them the piano.

It had been with them ever since. Where they went, the piano went.

All the same, we didn't see why it should cause quite so much trouble. After all, it wasn't as if anyone actually played it any more. What was more, it wasn't even allowed in Mother's and Father's sitting-room any longer.

'There just isn't *room*, you see,' Mother said. 'It just wouldn't fit in at all. Look at the colour scheme. I mean, you can see for yourself.'

It was one of those old, awkward contraptions, and you could never be quite sure you had got past it. There was always liable to be some unseen protuberance that caught the edge of your coat or poked you hard in the ribs.

Altogether, we felt that this ancient monstrosity should be forcibly retired. Between ourselves, in a rebellious mood, we would discuss selling it to a second-hand dealer, even giving it away. We were always badgering our friends, and even enemies, to see if they would like a nice, er, upright piano – lends tone, you know. Anything, in fact, to get rid of it.

Mind you, if ever we let the parents know what was in our minds, then the sparks would fly. Even Father would rouse himself from his pipe and his evening paper.

'Here now, you young folks. Show a bit o' respect for your elders.'

So the old piano just stood there in the hall, week after week. At last, in desperation, after nearly breaking our necks one night, my brother, Stan, and I moved it surreptitiously into young Johnny's room.

You should have heard the complaining when he woke up next morning! But we bribed him with some sweets and a few promises, and in the end he seemed to get used to it. He even strummed a few notes on it – a bit of Rock 'n' Roll.

Mother didn't like that: she complained at once. And anyway, modern stuff, like jazz and swing and boogie woogie, just didn't suit the old piano, you could sense that.

It was Johnny who, out of sheer devilment, got some paint and painted the old piano a bright buttercup yellow. My word, the fuss there was about that! But, in the end, it died down, and the piano remained where it was, in Johnny's room.

For a time life became easier. We really thought we'd solved the problem. And then young Johnny grew older, and joined the Merchant Navy, and Mother and Father found themselves with an empty room on their hands.

'Why not let it?' my brother Stan suggested.

'A good idea,' I told them.

We didn't think they would, but one night we came home and found Mother looking rather pleased with herself. Apparently she had let the room on the telephone to someone who had taken it on the spot. Mother hadn't bothered to mention the slight detail of the piano.

'But, Mother,' we protested, and tried to suggest darkly that there would be trouble about letting a room under false pretences.

'Nonsense,' she declared. 'I expect the gentleman will feel that the piano gives tone to the room. I mean, well – it's an asset, in its way.'

But she avoided meeting our gaze, and we knew that her doubts were there, waiting for the arrival of the new lodger.

When he arrived, he turned out to be a cheerful, tubby little man with white hair and spectacles. He seemed a nice little fellow by the name of Tomkins. He told me he preferred having a place of his own, rather than having to live in hotels.

'Here's your room,' Stan said, standing aside for Mr Tomkins to enter.

He stepped forward smartly, and then seemed to hesitate. We weren't really surprised. For all that my mother had tried to camouflage it with lace curtains and strips of cloth, the old piano dominated the room.

But we were misjudging our man. His hesitation, it transpired, was from pleasure, not shock. With a gasp of sheer delight, he positively scampered forward.

'A *piano*!' he said, almost in awe. 'How lovely! Would it be possible for me to play now and then?'

My mother, who had hovered nervously in the doorway, now came forward, beaming. 'But of course, Mr Tomkins.'

And she gave Stan and me a scornful look.

In a flash, Mr Tomkins had put down his suitcases and seated himself before the piano. Almost reverently, he lifted the bright yellow lid, and then those unfamiliar fingers, soon to be such intimate friends with our piano, began to spell out some old tunes.

Funny thing, but we'd never really heard the piano sound quite like that before. I mean, we'd all of us sometimes run our fingers up and down the keys, and, as I say, there was a time when Johnny fooled about a little. But this was, well, somehow different.

You know how it is when someone who really knows what they're doing takes over. We didn't know much about Mr Tomkins really, but in a few moments he showed us he knew something about pianos. It was something to do with the way he sat himself; something to do with the almost loving manner of his touch.

I must admit we were impressed. As for Mother, well, she was positively excited, hopping about from one foot to the other. I can see her now, with her eyes suddenly bright.

At last she asked Mr Tomkins if he knew some of her favourite tunes.

' "The Rose of Tralee" – do you remember?'

Mr Tomkins smiled. 'Very well. Very well, indeed.'

Mother clasped her hands together. 'And the other rose one – "Roses of Picardy." And – oh, then there's "Maid of the Mountains" … '

'But of course.' Mr Tomkins said, nodding his head vigorously. 'Would you like me to play them all?'

Mother nodded, and then lifted her hand, as if remembering something. 'Yes, please. But can you just wait a minute? I won't be very long.'

While Stan and I watched a little suspiciously. Mother rushed out of the room. We heard her running down the stairs, and the sitting-room door opening, and we guessed she had gone to fetch Father. Before long she was back, almost dragging a somewhat reluctant Father behind her.

'Now, Mr Tomkins,' my mother said, with a curious air of suppressed excitement in her voice. 'I think we're all ready. Do please play for us, will you?'

And Mr Tomkins played, at first rather softly, as if feeling his way, and then with growing confidence.

Strange, he was only a tubby little fellow, with white hair. Rather unprepossessing really, but my memory of him on this occasion is clear, indeed, vivid. His presence seemed somehow magnified. And after all, his presence was significant; he represented some slender, yet defininte link with the past.

And so, as I say, Mr Tomkins played. The tunes he played were old – positively ancient to Stan and me. The sort of light, romantic stuff that I had hardly ever heard of, let alone liked. 'Only a rose I bring thee.' 'Come, come, I love you only' – all that sort of stuff.

I don't know how long Mr Tomkins sat there, his white head bent forward, his spectacles bobbing up and down on his nose. It might have been five minutes or half an hour. I really couldn't tell.

After a while, Stan turned and looked at me. I think he was about to say something; but I shook my head, and then I nodded sideways. Taking his cue from me, Stan turned and looked across at Mother and Father.

Almost unconsciously they had drawn together, and Father had put one arm around Mother's shoulder, while she, for her part, was resting her grey head on his shoulder. They were swaying slightly with the old-fashioned lilt of the music.

After a while, Mother began humming the tunes, her rather fragile voice rising and falling with a curious sweetness against Mr Tomkins's music. I knew then that they were thirty years back in time, a young couple, who were miraculously in love for ever and ever. And before long I had to go out of the room with my brother Stan, or else I would have cried.

Funny thing, but since then none of us has ever complained about that old piano.

XX1

Life and Death Story

He was born in the middle of their interminable struggle. Indeed, from the moment of his conception he became a part of the struggle; belonging first to her, then to him, claimed from all angles, called upon, denied – tossed about like a legal argument that is polished and improved until it has become quite detached from its original source.

She had him in a hospital. Part of her would have preferred the familiarity of home, but there her husband's presence would have surrounded her, intruding persistently into this intimate process which she sought to establish as her own. So she went to the hospital, preferring all the antiseptic anonymity of the sterilized corridors, the white rooms, the spotless nurses.

When the actual birth took place, she gave herself up with strange pleasure to its compulsion. It was one experience she could indulge in as her own, divorced from that other exterior life – her own, secret, surpreme moment. The pain, the discomfort, even the final agony – nothing of that seemed to matter compared to her own fulfilment. She created, she fashioned, she was consummated. She delivered her son.

She awoke from her drowsy state, to find her infant suckling at her breast. The nurse leaned over, and smiled.

'Your husband is outside. He says he wants to see his son.'·

It was funny if it was not tragic. The woman wanted to laugh even as she wanted to cry. She would like to have been able to explain things to the nurse, to talk about it in some way. But it was something nobody could understand, only herself, only her husband. And now, perhaps her son? She looked curiously for a moment at the imcomprehensible bundle of new flesh and wizened skin. Incredible, unique, marvellous.

'Let him in,' she said wearily.

When her husband came in his eyes sought the hump in the bedclothes, the newcomer. He approached without a word, and stood looking down at the strange shape. He looked for so long, so unblinkingly, that the woman felt more and more exasperated. In the end she could stand it no longer.

'He's hungry. I must feed him.'

And authoritatively, possessively, she turned the wizened head towards her succulent breasts, and the greedy lips opened and closed. Ah, thought the woman, what a beautiful sensation, what a delicate and intimate sensation, my son's lips upon my breasts. And the ecstasy of her experience must have suffused her face with contentment.

The man could not bear to see her expression; and yet manners demanded something from him. He cleared his throat, and looked about uncomfortably.

'Did you have a bad time? Was it … '

He looked at the woman, and she eyed him steadily. Only they understood the reality of such looks, all the secret inviolable tensions and challenges.

She shrugged. 'It wasn't so bad. I had some stitches. But I'm all right.'

'Yes,' said the man, almost bitterly. 'I can see you're all right.'

And he stared again at the child. 'Difficult to tell who he's like.'

The woman smiled secretively. 'Oh, I don't know … '

'Come, come,' said the man loudly. 'You don't mean to tell me you can tell a likeness now? Why, its impossible.'

The woman shrugged. And in her shrug she answered, 'Don't be foolish, it is quite possible. He is my son, he looks like me.'

'Oh, you women!' said the man angrily, half looking at the nurse. 'You're always so confident.' He made a gesture. 'We must wait and see.'

But obviously he felt impotent, rather helpless. Obviously he was on the wrong battleground. And soon he went away again leaving the woman momentarily happy, yet fearful for the future. She nestled her son's curly head against her cheek and whispered endearments into his ears. She tried not to think about the time when she would be home, the three of them alone, and ... then?

Their attraction had been one of antagonism from the start. Each had resented and sought to master the other. Neither had succeeded. So the struggle was permanent, unending, inconclusive. Even their love-making was as much a struggle as pleasure. Conquest was pain, pain was conquest – everything had been hopelessly mixed up from the beginning. Neither of them quite knew where they stood. They wandered about in a morass of quicksands, clinging to each other in desperation, merely to save themselves.

When they found a child was coming each was secretly relieved. This, they felt, would crystallize matters, this would be a turning point – this would divide or unite, some sort of pattern would be formulated.

But it did not happen like that. When the woman and child came home, when they were established again in the routine of the semi-detached house, its suburban regularity, the struggle continued. The battle was not ended but intensified. And now the spoils were displayed.

During the day she had the boy to herself, it was true. Each morning, as her husband walked away to catch his train to the city, she felt a glorious sense of freedom. She turned from the window and held her hands out and picked up the boy and swung him round in an abandoned way.

'My baby! My little baby! Come to your mummy!'

And she would press the soft bundle of flesh and bones against her cheek, loving the warmth and softness – her warmth and softness. All day she would be almost happy because almost forgetting her husband, his part in her life, in their life.

But as evening approached, she dreaded hearing the gate click, his measured footsteps. Most of all she dreaded the moment when the door handle rattled and automatically, excitedly, the baby's large brown eyes peered towards the door, the tiny familiar mouth pouting its expectant welcome.

'Well!' he would cry, throwing open the door, 'how is my little son today?'

And then the moment would be his, the embrace his, the ecstasy his: and she hated him for it. She wished he were anywhere else, she wished he did not exist. It was all she could do to stop herself seizing the child from him, physically parting the ridiculous, unwarranted partnership. For he was her son, hers. She had borne him, had conceived and endured and brought into the world this tiny, lovable object. What right had her husband to possess him? None!

And thinking thus, exhibiting all her feelings, she provoked her husband into fresh irritation. He felt compelled to exaggerate his own behaviour towards the child.

'Ah, my son! You're a little wonder! Look how bright his eyes are, my little son.'

Always son, always my son. From both of them the attack was direct, relentless. Their marriage indeed now had its focal point. Here, squatting brightly on the carpet between them, existed the fusion point of all their struggles. My son, my son, O Absalom.

He grew up watched, beloved, bedevilled perhaps. Every day, every hour, every moment, he was in their minds. They searched avidly to find some new facet, some new endearment or habit, with which they could associate themselves. They vied with each other to claim likenesses, similarities – see, this habit is mine, that gurgle was mine. It would have been funny were it not so deadly in earnest. Between them they dissected and examined him a dozen times a day. It was largely fortuitous that they should put him together again, that he should remain whole for so long.

But that they did not consider. They were too busy engaged on their private war. And perhaps, who knows, in some curious way enjoying themselves. For their lives were relatively uncomplicated. External events seldom intruded. It was enough that he had a steady job, that she was an efficient housewife. They had a pleasant home, the weeks ticked by rhythmically. All else was subordinated to the one life that they had created between them. Or, as it would seem each maintained despite the other.

When the baby was two, he became somehow a boy. This was the woman's loss. Some indescribable feminine bond was broken. For a long time, unwilling to admit defeat, she persisted in dressing him as a baby, with big bows, frilly dresses. Until one day they had a furious row about it, and the man shouted at her.

'You're trying to turn him into a girl! I won't have it. You shan't!'

And though she shouted back, she knew that she couldn't alter the course of nature. He was no girl, he was no baby, either. He was manifestly a boy – curly-haired, round-faced, bright-eyes, a boy. Her son. No, said the man's proud eyes, my son.

He grew. His hair was cut short. His legs were longer. He went to a kindergarten, dressed smartly, rather prettily. He sat at desks, he looked at blackboards, he met other children, other parents. The world began to assume large shapes, more mysteries. He grew older, wiser, he was the schoolboy.

They watched him from their vantage points, marvelling, wondering, scheming. Sometimes they took him out together, more often they took him out separately. Alone, having him completely to their selfish selves, they poured out their stories, they weaved their webs.

She took him out in the daytime, plying him with ice creams and lemonade, sitting in a cafe and watching indulgently as he ate himself almost sick.

'Are you happy, my son? Is there anything you want? Anything? Remember, your mother loves you. She will always look after you.'

And the time passed in a wallow of sentimentality, while the boy consumed doughnut after doughnut, ice cream upon ice cream.

When his father took him out, it was week-ends, or evenings, rather special occasions. Secretly, naturally, the boy preferred those outings. They went to football matches, to boxing tournaments. Through his son his father relived his own youth. His voice was gay as he described, explained, embroidered. The occasions became alive and excitable and the boy showed his obvious enjoyment.

Then perhaps the mother would become angry, yet she had her many weapons, her strings to pull. In pain, in trouble, in fright, it was to his mother that the boy turned. In the dark night, in the grey morning, awakening from some nightmare, he would seek those familiar arms, that familiar breast.

Then the father would cloak his jealousy with anger.

'Don't pander to the boy. Don't mollycoddle him! He will grow up a baby, a coward.'

And hearing such words, the boy would shrink from his father, he would curl into his mother's arms, as he had once curled into her womb.

Yet there was no end to the seesaw. For did not the boy delight now in walking with his father to the station, in helping his father mend the car, in playing games in the garden?

Oh, it was infinite, the tug of war, the tension, the endless skirmishing. They seemed tireless in the struggle. In some way they almost seemed to feed and thrive upon each day's events, each stage of the battle. A victory was heartening, a defeat was challenging.

The husband and the wife, indeed, thrived. But the son did not. Like some hothouse flower, too much cared for, too delicately treated, he wilted. Not immediately. Not even noticeably. But secretly, subtly, and in a deadly fashion.

At first his mother and father did not notice. And then, as the familiar limbs grew thinner, the beloved face gaunt, as the eyes filled less and less with light and more and more with death – then they could not fail to notice. My son, you are not well! You need medical care, you need looking after …

In the moment of alarm, still they remained apart. They were untiring in their care, in their attention – they were ceaseless in their hours of loving nursing. But they sat separately, or on opposite sides of the bed. Each knew better than the other. Each had a different diagnosis, a different treatment. Each took the doctor's grave words, translated them differently, used them mainly as weapons against the other.

'You have smothered the boy with your mothering! See what you have done to him!'

'Nonsense! It is you. Imposing yourself, bullying the child. You have threatened him. It is you – you!'

And enraged they stared at each other, across the bed, over the sleeping boy.

Sleep seemed to be his escape from them. Sometimes his eyes might open and look at one or the other. Father, mother, who were they? He looked at them blankly, as if they were denizens of another world, as indeed already they were. They stared at him fiercely. Oh, my son, oh, my little boy! But he saw them as apparitions that had never entered his world, and he returned gratefully to his own fantasies.

A few weeks later he died. There was nothing dramatic about his death, as perhaps they would have liked. There were no violent deathbed scenes, no reconciliations or accusations. In fact he died quietly in his sleep, and no one knew anything about it for some time. He lay there, quiet and still, as he had lain for months, a faint smile on his pallid lips. He had just stopped breathing, that was all.

Their anguish was immediate. Their misery swept over them with equal force. Alone with each other, they could not bear to comfort each other, nor yet to be apart. They sniffled and bemoaned, they pitied themselves, and then him. Somehow they got through the occasion, somehow they endured the time till the funeral, till the small coffin was lowered reverently, finally, into the solid earth.

Then it was all over. They turned and walked slowly home. They were together, and yet apart. As always. And yet, perhaps, wasn't there, didn't there? Secretly, their thoughts wound ahead. Furtively they eyed each other. Yes, there was no denying it. A bond between them had been established once and for all. For the rest of their lives, they could not forget him, could not obliterate him. Time, eternity, nothing could remove his having existed. Always he would hover over their shoulders, symbol of something that had belonged neither to one nor the other, and yet to both. He was their son, their own son. In his existence he had symbolized everything that they had secretly tried to deny.

It was an awful thought. They banished it from their minds. But they knew it would return. They knew the course of their lives had been settled. Inescapably, now, they were man and wife, father and mother. They went back to the suburban house. He resumed his work, she resumed her work. Life went on as before. But now they had an easier subject of conversation. In death he became more real than in life. And somehow more peaceful, more mellowing. With the years their memories would interfuse, their arguments interlock. Until gradually, under his rosy aura, beholden to his sentimentalized memory – out of their own selfishness – they might even grow fond of one another. So, they would conclude, his life was not really wasted after all, was it?

XXII

Before the Event

The extraordinary sense of apprehension, a kind of fearful awareness of some terrible impending experience, first came upon Robert Carrington when he was driving home from his town office one summer evening. He lived in one of those outlying areas which gave a faint illusion of being almost in the country, while yet enabling the journey from house to office to be made in just under an hour. Now, on this evening, he had at last broken free of the endless traffic jams and was heading at some speed along the last few miles of comparatively open roadway. At the last minute, reaching the 40 mile speed limit sign at the entrance to his village, he slowed down, then swung round a sharp bend into the tree-lined avenue that eventually led to his own semi-detached home. On the way he waved to some of the neighbours – old Mr Pengelly bent diligently over his herbaceous border, the Taylors sitting in deck-chairs on their verandah, the Elliot boys having a game of clock golf, pretty little Nelly Hoskins playing some game with a ball on her father's newly tarmaced drive. It was that sort of place, a little genteel and middle-class, pleasant enough, too. In all the ten years he had lived and prospered there Robert Carrington had never known anything really untoward to happen.

This was what made the unfamiliar mood of depression which seemed to have overcome him more unusual. When he had set out he had felt as he generally felt a little tired from a hard day at the office, looking forward to getting home as quickly as possible and relaxing with a gin and tonic before the evening meal. By the time he finally turned the car into the garage, he was pale and trembling, and filled with a most alarming feeling of dread.

Sitting in the car, trying to compose himself before attempting to make a normal entry into the family fold, he sought for some explanation. He had felt all right driving out along the by-pass. It had been later on, as he neared the end of his journey, that the strange feeling had begun. At first it had just been a niggling thing, an irritating sense of worry. But what had he been worrying about? It couldn't have been the driving, the road was clear, there had been surprisingly little traffic coming up to the village. The day's events at the office – no, nothing there to be worried about. Something waiting for him at home? – but no, that was ridiculous, all that awaited was pleasant, a quick gin and tonic, dinner with his wife and two children, maybe watching television afterwards ...

Then what? For there was no doubt about it, the worry had grown, had turned into very real apprehension – indeed, just as he reached the village he had experienced a blinding moment of outright fear, so that it had been all he could do to prevent himself stopping the car there and then. Instead, cross with himself, he had driven on and up to the house and into the garage. After a while the memory of that terrible moment had dimmed: but he was left with the persistent apprehension, no doubt about that. It hung all around him, like a dull ache. At last, realizing he was not going to be able to will it away, he shrugged wearily, and took it with him into the house.

Although he did his best to pretend nothing was wrong, his wife sensed the nervousness, and persuaded him to have an extra drink, which was probably a good idea as it enabled him to get through the evening meal in a fairly natural manner. Then, sitting watching television, he was able to delude himself that he was beginning to escape from the mood. But by the time the play was over and the kids had gone to bed and his wife had shut the television off and they stretched their legs before going up to bed, he knew that things were just as bad as ever.

'What on earth's wrong?' said his wife. 'You look quite washed out.'

'I know.'

He hesitated, wishing he could explain, as much for his own

sake as hers. Suddenly he had a strange desire to get up and
walk over to the windows of the sitting room which looked out
upon the tree-lined avenue. Out there, he knew everything was
quiet and peaceful ... yet, almost immediately, he became
aware of an underlying sense of – well, menace was the only
word for it. Menace.

With a quick, unnatural movement he grasped the curtains
and drew them right across, blocking out the cool night air.

His wife looked round in astonishment.

'Why did you do that?'

He shook his head.

'I don't know. I just felt ... '

'Oh, really! It's so terribly hot!'

Not taking him seriously, she got up and parted the curtains
again. She stood there for a moment savouring the sweet
smells of fragrance from the garden. With his back still turned
away her husband said gruffly.

'What's – what's it like out there?'

'Like? Why you know what it's like – it's a lovely cool
summer evening. Robert, what *is* the matter?'

'I don't know ... '

He shook his head, still turned away. He knew that he was
afraid to turn back to face the window and whatever lay
outside, intangible and illusory though it might be.

Mumbling something, he went off to bed. By the time his
wife had joined him he was curled up in a corner, inviolate,
obviously wanting to be left alone. She hoped he would fall
asleep quickly and feel better in the morning. If not she might
try and persuade him to take a day off from the office. His
nerves really did seem on edge.

Over the next few days Robert Carrington's nerves became
very much more on edge. Others beside his family began to
notice it. People at the office. 'Don't want to be nosy, old boy,'
said his boss, 'but are you having a spot of domestic trouble or
anything? You look ghastly.' Neighbours, too. Old Mr
Pengelly commented that he looked proper parched, and their
close friends the Taylors suggested he needed a holiday. Even

little Nelly Hoskins, who was almost invariably playing about outside her house when he came back, came dancing after him one night and called out gaily. 'Don't worry, Mr Carrington, it may never happen!' – and skipped away again, like a pretty young fairy.

God, he thought safe in the seclusion of the garage, where he had taken to spending a while each evening regaining his composure, is it as obvious as all that? One day he buried his face in his hands as if trying to obliterate strange visions. But when he raised his face again, as though there were visions (although there never were) the *Feeling* remained.

It was the feeling which worried him most of all, which was the most difficult thing to explain to anyone like his wife, or even the doctor he eventually went to see.

'It's just that I have this awful sense of – well, blame, you might say – or guilt, perhaps. I don't know how to put it, Doctor, but often when I'm walking about in the village I have the strangest feeling … as if people are watching me, accusingly – blaming me for something – something awful. But – I don't know what it is, do you see? That's the terrible thing.'

There, he had managed in a way to express it with a certain degree of clarity. But, alas, the doctor, naturally enough, simply saw it as a pretty straightforward case of anxiety complex and nervous tension.

'I shouldn't worry too much, Mr Carrington. It's fairly common these days, especially among business people. Nothing serious, I can assure you. I'll prescribe some pills that will bring quite a lot of relief, I think you'll find.'

Possibly pills might have helped, but somehow Robert Carrington could not persuade himself to take them. He knew they would simply be tranquillizers of some kind, and he feared that their sole effect would be to lull his troubled sense into a state of false security. By now he was quite convinced that there must be some other answer to his problem. So he took the pills home, put them in a cupboard, and left them there.

He began, each day, trying to grapple with his problem. He knew it was growing to alarming proportions because already he was reaching a stage where he found himself making excuses for not going out anywhere – not into the village, not for an outing, not even to visit neighbours.

'Robert, what is it? What's wrong? Please tell me,' said his wife. Her look of sadness touched him deeply. It was as if – and this frightened him even more – as if there was an implied recognition that already he was beyond her help.

'Oh, my dear,' he exclaimed, unbearably moved! 'Oh, my dearest!'

And he embraced his wife suddenly, fearfully, as if almost afraid to let her go again.

'Robert,' she said gently at last. 'You really must have a rest or a change or something.'

'A rest?' he said vaguely. 'A change?' He frowned, and shook his head. It would be no good; he would go away, and come back, and it would all start again. He felt sure of that. But what?

What indeed? From the time he drove off from the house in the morning until he finally lay in bed at night, unable to sleep, listening for strange sounds, he strove desperately to find some explanation. There was something, something awful, and he was no nearer to knowing what it was than on that first day when the mood caught up with him. Not that he was under any delusions about it being a passing mood. It was something with him, he knew, for a long time – perhaps, he sometimes thought anguishedly, until his dying day.

But what? After a while other people began asking, becoming worried. He shrank awkwardly from their questions just as, he had noticed, he was tending to shrink more and more from human contacts around him. It was as if – as if there were already some greater menace about such contacts. And worse, he came to have the feeling that these contacts in themselves might involve some sort of risk, exposing him to public disapproval. Yes, that was it ... Suddenly one day, driving home, just as he reached the familiar village signs, he had a clear, almost blinding awareness of other people's dislike. Or rather, more than that, a kind of *hatred*. He drove home that night without daring to look right or left, not acknowledging the usual greeting, afraid that he might recognize something of the hidden, swelling antagonism.

It was a terrible new knowledge that he now took with him everywhere: the fact that all around him there existed some very real kind of mounting dislike for himself. Not just the dislike of a single person, either, but of many – perhaps, for all he knew, of the whole community.

He wished he could have tried to talk about it, to explain what he felt to someone. Surely he could speak to his own wife? One evening, desperately, he tried to bring himself to do so: but then, irrationally, he found himself remembering that evening when he had sensed the lurking antagonism outside and had drawn the curtains, and how, without considering his feelings, she had drawn back the curtains, exposing him to the unknown. No, he could not even talk to his own wife.

It was at this stage, perhaps not surprisingly, that Robert Carrington began drinking. He had always been a drinker in what might be called moderation. Now he began drinking a great deal, indeed most immoderately. Despite the fact that it obviously affected his office work, he began drinking in the lunch hour, sometimes three or four whiskies. When he got home in the evening he took to slipping in a couple of quick extra drinks when his wife wasn't about.

Finally, he discovered the extra benefit of a drink or two on the way home from work: there were several quite pleasant pubs … He was not drinking for drinking's sake, by any means. The fact was that, through all the faint haze created by his general drinking, he had become aware of a steady and quite terrifying magnification of his fears and apprehensions. For some reason he was finding it more and more difficult to bring himself to set off on that hour's journey home. Sometimes he had to literally force himself to get into the car, switch on the ignition key, and start for home. The feeling of desolation, of impending disaster – even of some kind of doom – was so strong now that if it had not been for the newly discovered alleviation offered by his pub calls he knew that he might never have completed the journeys. So he had one whisky and soda at this pub, and a second at that pub, and a third ... and in due course a fourth at a pub nearer to home. And each evening the drinks served to give him some kind of momentary courage, so that there were even times when he might pluck up courage enough to nod briefly to Mr Pengelly, to wave to the Taylors, to nod at the Elliot boys, even to catch an approving glimpse of little Nelly Hoskins in her pink dress chasing her bright yellow ball ...

But then he had only been back in his house a short while when the Dutch courage was gone, and he began to suffer afterthoughts: about the way old Mr Pengelly eyed him, the way the Taylors had seemed not to wave back, how the Elliot boys had seemed to ignore his call ... And Nelly Hoskins? Had she just gone on playing? Or what had she done? He struggled hard, in the dark hours of the night, as if in some way the absurd solution might answer all his other questions, to remember what Nelly had done with that bright yellow ball?

The next evening, sunshine bathing everywhere in a glow of well being, Robert Carrington came driving home from his office. He had drunk rather more than usual during the day, so that his extra drinks on the drive home were more potent than normal. Driving rather fast – for he knew himself to be an experienced and thoroughly reliable driver – Robert Carrington swept into his familiar village at a speed considerably beyond the prescribed 30 miles per hour. With a wild screech of brakes he managed to swing round the corner of the familiar tree-lined avenue, and then roared at a totally unsuitable speed down towards his own house.

Like a man in a daze he failed to see the startled greeting of old Mr Pengelly, the suddenly perturbed waves of the Taylors, the half formed warning cry of one of the Elliot boys – or the last minute rolling to safety, on the other side of the road, of the bright yellow ball. He did not see, but felt with every agonized nerve in his body, the dull thud as the steel-grilled bonnet of his car hit the happy, laughing pink-dressed memory of Nelly Hoskins, and hurled her into eternity.

'You mad devil!' cried a voice.

'That poor little girl — is she?'

'I'm afraid so. Will someone call an ambulance?'

'And the police ... '

'As for that drunken swine ... '

'He ought to be lynched ... '

And sitting slumped helplessly over the wheel of his finally silent car – too late, oh, too late, too late? – Robert Carrington recognized at last the awful and terrible truth.

It was all just beginning.

XXIII

The Portrait

Ladies and gentlemen of the jury, the defence in this case, which I am conducting myself, is based entirely upon a single item which stands in front of you – a portrait painted in oils on a canvas measuring some three feet by two feet, and framed in deal wood and glass. It is, as you can see for yourselves, a figurative work in traditional style, painted about ten years ago. The likeness is an extraordinarily close one: and the portrait, of course, is of my wife.

I should like first, if I may, to sketch in something of the background of this portrait. It was commissioned by me as a wedding anniversary gift to my wife, at a not insubstantial fee. The artist, Mr Frederick O'Brien, in addition to being an esteemed member of his profession, was a personal friend, and had indeed illustrated several of my own books. I mention this to demonstrate that we were on familiar terms so that it seemed the most natural thing in the world, when I decided to commission a painting of my wife, that I should entrust the task to Mr O'Brien. He agreed with enthusiasm and began work immediately, though I think it is extremely relevant to mention that the total time which elapsed between the artist starting and finishing the portrait was one year. Upon reflection you may feel, as I did myself, that this is rather a longer time than one would normally expect to be devoted to a single portrait.

Nevertheless, the portrait was finally completed and presented – to the pleasure not only of my wife and myself but also of a large circle of friends and acquaintances. Everyone was most impressed and I can remember how frequently I was congratulated on having the foresight to pick such a talented artist to paint my wife's portrait. Although perhaps not entirely appropriate to the matter under discussion I think it is fair to say that this work – which of course I was pleased to lend out for a number of art exhibitions – helped very considerably in the furtherance of Mr O'Brien's career.

Ladies and gentlemen of the jury, I should now like to draw your attention to the content of this portrait. It is, as I have said, a picture of my wife, but I hope you will agree it is also the image of a very beautiful woman. That graceful swan-like neck, those smooth, pearl-white shoulders, the gently flushed cheek, above all those luminous green eyes, as deep and mysterious as the ocean itself – they were all those attributes of my wife's loveliness which had long been my delight. Why, even the golden hair, coiling in long careless strands down her back to give her an appearance of a Rossetti model – even this the painter assiduously copied, with loving care. Yes, it is quite a miraculous example of reality translated into life upon the canvas.

But as I was saying, to the content. The portrait reflects this lovely lady, my wife, seated serenely and composed and looking out upon the world – it is obvious that the painter determined to capture the whole essence and being of his subject, and there can be little doubt that he succeeded. Here is the whole woman – indeed, if you like to generalise, here is Woman. Vivid and alive, of infinite mood and caprice, a colourful and striking example of feminine beauty, once seen, never to be forgotten.

Yes, I think we may agree that artistically the portrait is most impressive … and if there are any doubts on this point I can easily call expert witnesses to testify in my support. However, the burden of my case rests not on the technical skill of the portrait but rather on some more intangible aspect – would that I could indeed call experts to back me in this sphere, but, alas, I cannot.

Ladies and gentlemen of the jury, I want you now to try and put yourselves in my position. I am happily married, I have an excellent job, every evening I return from my office to a gracious home – usually I sink into my favourite armchair in the lounge, sipping a glass of whisky before dinner – and almost inevitably I look across the room at this portrait of my wife, hanging in solitary splendour in the middle of the opposite wall. In the subdued lighting of the room somehow the figure and personality of my wife often seem to emerge more strongly than ever. How vibrant with life: how warm and glowing: – above all, how physically sensuous and sensual – how damned attractive! Why, it is almost too good to be true.

What I am trying to explain is that very gradually – and you must, of course, bear in mind that I looked at this portrait every day of my life for many years – I began to be disturbed. In fact, the portrait began to be an obsession, dominating my thoughts continually. For it seemed to me that every evening when I sat down and looked at it, so I perceived yet another shadowy glimpse of – something wrong. For a long time I could not put my finger on any particular aspect, yet I knew things were somehow not as they should be.

One evening, in a blinding flash, I realised what was the matter. This beautiful, sensual woman, sitting there with her white shoulders so provocatively bared, her long golden hair blowing wild and free; this woman with the great green eyes burning with secret passion – she was not just a meek wife dutifully sitting for a portrait. Oh, no – she was altogether too alive, too bursting with emotion – an emotion that was undisguised, to say the least. Why, in those bold features was a clear expression of a frank curiosity, indeed a passionate awareness ...

But not for her husband! That was the great truth that dawned on me after so long a time. It had been too simple for me to sit back in my chair night after night and assume casually that the woman in the portrait, my own wife, was smiling at me, her husband. It was not like that at all. The woman in the portrait was leaning forward in all her physical provoca-tiveness, and smiling tantalisingly – in surroundings of evident intimacy and secrecy – at the man who was painting her.

I need not burden you here with the details of how night after night I continued to confirm and strengthen my theory –

save to mention that every time I looked more closely, so I found new strands with which to weave together this damning indictment. Gradually I began to realise that there were many faithful touches put in by the artist which only served to emphasise an aura of illicit passion and deceit – even, one felt, of impending, perhaps immediate unfaithfulness.

Yes, indeed, my friends, it should not really be difficult, if you have managed to put yourselves in my unfortunate position, for you to understand how finally and logically I came to realise the real truth of the matter ... that I was no longer looking at my wife, but at a wanton woman of the world, at an adulteress – at the mistress of Frederick O'Brien.

It has been difficult in mere words to convey to you the mesmeristic effect of those evenings by the fire. I can remember how I began sitting there, not for a few moments as before, but for an hour or more, drinking whisky after whisky, staring all the time at that ever-changing phantasm, with such ferocious intensity that sometimes indeed the portrait appeared to cease being a portrait, becoming instead almost alive, almost a real woman ...

Finally there came a night when my wife, entering the room rather unexpectedly, appeared in some strange way to merge into the portrait itself so that it was difficult to tell one from the other, one beautiful false wanton creature from the other. Such was the hypnotic effect of the moment that I was unable to restrain the flood of tangled emotions that rose up in me. Suddenly I found myself accusing my wife of everything that I had been suspecting – of having been unfaithful to me, of having had an affair with Frederick O'Brien during that year when he was working on the painting ...

Ladies and gentlemen of the jury, I must now conclude by telling you that, caught off her guard, my wife freely admitted that everything hinted at by the aspect of her image in the portrait was in fact true – and I think you will surely agree that in the blinding heat of such a moment, distraught to the point of madness by this revelation of unfaithfulness, I might have been pardoned for giving vent to my most primitive feelings, and strangling my wife with my bare hands there and then.

Instead, I have to confess, I took down the portrait, smashed the frame, and tore the painting into several fragments, which you now see before you cunningly re-assembled into a passable impression of the original.

Ladies and gentlemen of the jury, in view of the above circumstances I confidently appeal to you to dismiss the legal action brought by my wife against me for alleged damage to her personal property. Thank you.